Cigarette

Per Hagman
CIGARETTE

Translated by Elinor Fahrman

nordisk books

Published by Nordisk Books, 2022
www.nordiskbooks.com

© 1991 Per Hagman
First published by Albert Bonnier, Sweden
Published by arrangement with Nordin Agency AB, Sweden

English translation © Elinor Fahrman

Cover design © Nordisk Books

Printed and bound in Great Britain by Clays Ltd, Elcograf S.p.A.

A CIP catalogue record for this book is available from the British Library

ISBN 9781838074289
eBook ISBN 9781838074296

'…and then we were in Ios and it was so fucking cheap you couldn't really say no… there was just so much fucking puffing,' says Micke and smiles and Fredrik has a go on the balloon and starts talking in a Donald Duck voice and I light a match to give me something to do. "Micke pick-up" is called out from the kitchen loud speakers and he quickly drinks the last of the coffee and leaves the room. Fredrik has another go on the helium and asks in his Donald Duck voice:

'Are you working tomorrow?'

'Mmm, lunch,' I say.

'So you're not coming out tonight then?' His voice returns to normal halfway through the sentence.

'No, I don't think so.'

'Fuck this gas is making me feel really sick.' He takes a sip of juice.

I finish around eleven and when I come home I watch the last ten minutes of some thriller and go to bed.

It's a pretty nice day at work. A decent number of guests and nice staff. When it's calmed down after lunch, me and a new waiter called Anders play pinball. The balls run straight through but it doesn't matter. We play for an hour or so and there isn't a single guest in the restaurant. When the coins run out we go downstairs to the kitchen to blag some ice cream. The whole afternoon calmly passes by and I'm home around half six. Had planned to do the laundry but as soon as I sit down I fall asleep.

Wake up half nine by someone banging hysterically at the door.

'What the fuck are you doing?' Tobbe laughs when I finally open. 'I've been knocking on your door for fifteen minutes.'

I clear my throat and splutter something about having just woken up.

'Woken up? I thought we were going out tonight? I brought two bottles of wine.' He's in high spirits and asks cheerfully if I've spoken to Viktor or Micke and I say that I'd completely forgotten we were going anywhere.

'Haven't even been to the liquor store.'

I get a plastic bag from the kitchen and start clearing the table in front of the TV. An old yoghurt tub with some kind of insect in it, empty crisp packets, bottle tops with cigarette buts in them. The ashtrays are overflowing and it clearly looks like shit. Tobbe gets two glasses and opens one of the bottles. I turn on the TV. Cable is showing a gig with some band and I leave it on. Call Viktor but it's busy and I call Micke but his answering machine says he's at mine.

'How was it today then?' Tobbe asks.

'Ok... Best day in a while actually.'

'That new waitress... what's her name... you know... was she working?'

'No.' I have a sip of wine. 'Why? Are you interested, or... what?' I smile and he smiles back and says 'Hard Rock Café, love all... you know.'

We're quiet and I light a cigarette and watch that band on the TV. The singer is bald and wears shades. Behind the stage there is a gigantic screen showing blurry old war photos. I'm wondering if the photos have something to do with the song or if they're only there because it looks cool.

'Where are we going tonight then?' Tobbe asks.

'Patricia?' I suggest.

'Maybe baby,' he says and smiles and runs both hands through his short bleached hair.

I call Viktor again who says he's up for going out.

'You don't happen to have a spare bottle of wine? I'll pay you?' I ask.

'I might do, I owe you one or two anyway... I'll be over in twenty minutes or so.'

When I've hung up I hear Micke arriving.

'Well hello you old dopeheads, how's it going?' He holds up a bag and the bottles clang. 'The door was open... so...'

I swap to MTV and turn the sound up. There's a Def Leppard video on. "Pour some sugar on me, come on and fly me in…"

Micke opens an Old Gold and stands in front of us at the table and nearly downs the whole thing. He puts the bottle down and burps smiling and beer runs down his chin and onto his shirt, some trendy red paisley thing. He lights a cigarette and sits down. Tobbe opens his second bottle of wine and pours me a glass.

'So you've already started I see. Where are we off to then?'

'Patricia?' I say.

'Patricia?'

'Yes.'

'Not on a Wednesday for fuck's sake. It's totally dead.'

'You come up with something then.'

'Melody?'

'Melody?'

'Yes.'

'Let's just see where we end up,' Tobbe chips in.

There seems to be some Def Leppard special on the TV. That song "Women" comes on. Micke says this one is so fucking good and Tobbe says meh. I'm wondering if it was the drummer of Def Leppard that lost his arm in a car accident but I can't be bothered asking and flick to Teletext to find out what time it is. Twenty-three minutes past ten. I get up and walk over to open a window. Light a cigarette and look down on Västmannagatan. Hear Micke tell a detailed story of a movie scene where a girl is giving a dog a blowjob at the same time as some bloke is whipping the dog whilst having a wank and another bloke is watching him and having a wank. I go back to the table and sit down and pour another glass.

Viktor arrives with four bottles of wine. He asks how far in we are and Micke says he's on his fourth or fifth beer.

'Better hurry up then.' He pulls a corkscrew out of his pocket and smiles. Viktor looks splendidly correct in his white shirt and black tie and expensive thick corduroys. Probably has something to do with him being a secretary or something at some law firm.

After a while we're all quite wasted and Micke and Tobbe are deep in conversation about the sex scene in "Hotel St Pauli." Viktor who's seated opposite me lights a cigarette and says:

'It sucks really.'

'What does?' I ask and wonder if I just smoked or if I should light a new one.

'Everything really, for fuck's sake Johan…'

It sounds like the start of an embarrassing and annoying discussion but luckily Tobbe interrupts and suggests we leave. I down the last of the wine.

We end up at Melody around half twelve after randomly crossing half the town in cabs. The dance floor is overcrowded. "Goodlife" by Innercity is playing insanely loud. Viktor starts talking to a girl I think I recognise. Micke and Tobbe are talking to the barman and I go upstairs. I feel drunk. Say hi to a girl I talked to at some party. She doesn't reply. On the stairs I bump into a girl who's studying journalism at the university. She often hangs out at Tranan and I've spoken to her a few times before. I come up with some cliché like, Fancy seeing you here, and she laughs and says you seem a bit drunk. She's wearing a black vest and the disc jockey is playing "Love Action" and I think I'm horny. We sit down at a table on the stairs next to another couple and the guy is wearing a gigantic ear ring and the girl drinks Stella straight from the bottle and looks bored. The disc jockey plays "Don't You Want Me" and this journalist girl says great they're playing so many old songs and I nod and then ask how she could tell I was drunk and she says you can tell by the eyes and I hope she'll ask me what my name is so I can then ask her even though I don't really care. Micke comes past and shouts "shag" in my ear and I shake my head slightly embarrassed and I hope she didn't hear. She says what's your name by the way and I say Johan what about you? Nina, she says and I nod and smile. She smiles. I look down on the dance floor and see Viktor dancing with that girl who I still can't place. Still, I wouldn't have minded shagging her.

'Do you want to go down to the bar,' I ask and she says yes, I think I'll have a beer.

On the way down we bump into Micke again and he says he and Tobbe and some people from Monarch are off to a club in Apelbergsgatan and I say have fun and he smiles and says you too.

Nina orders a San Miguel and I have a glass of white. She drinks straight from the bottle and I watch. I like watching her neck when she swallows. I think I should ask her about her studies and she says she finishes in three weeks and that she's got a job at DN over the summer. Realise it sounds ridiculous when I say, ah, well, I subscribe to DN. She lights a cigarette and says it's twenty to three. I also light a cigarette and we watch the dance floor quietly for a minute or two. Finally she suggests we should leave before the cloakroom gets rammed.

When we get our clothes she asks if we should get a cab to Röda Rummet over by Norra Bantorget and I say sure, I'm pretty hungry.

It's not particularly busy when we arrive. The three am rush probably hasn't started. I buy two sandwiches and a coffee from the Turkish guy (Greek? Iranian?) by the till. Nina has a juice. We sit down in a corner by the window and I look out at the street whilst I eat. A taxi has just stopped outside. A dark-haired guy who's been sitting in the front seat gets out but bends down and says something to the driver. I can make out a girl in the back seat counting money. Another guy with longish hair and a leather jacket, who's been sitting next to the girl, gets out the other side. He goes around the car and grabs hold of the guy talking to the driver. He shouts something at him and then they both start laughing. The girl gets out and they enter the café but I don't want to turn around and look at them.

The second sandwich isn't as good as the first one and I end up leaving half. A last sip of coffee and then I light a cigarette. Feel a bit under pressure as we haven't said anything to each other for probably five minutes, so I ask if she wants to come back to mine and she says yes. We go out into the street and get a cab straight away. It's started raining and I love being in a cab at night in the rain. We're both in the back seat and when it turns into Dalagatan I kiss her.

We come back to mine and I want to fuck her straight away but Nina (was it Nina? Lina?) goes into the kitchen and I hear her say it could do with tidying up.

'Do you have tea?'

'Tea?'

'Yes, tea?'

'Erm… I guess.'

I don't like this but she puts the kettle on and smiles at me. There's a Camel Light on the kitchen table that I pick up and start smoking. We sit down but I get up again and go into the living room and turn on the cable channel. There's a video with Michael Jackson and it's pretty bad but I turn the sound up and go back into the kitchen and sit down. I really didn't think she was this type, tea, candles, the meaning of life and all that.

Whilst we're drinking tea she tries to come up with loads of annoying things to say. I am quiet and try to answer in as few words as possible when she says something. Finally, I pluck up the courage to say I'm tired and go to the loo. Give the mirror a psychopathic stare and whisper shag to myself. Wash my face in cold water and dry myself thoroughly. I leave the loo and she goes in. I undress. Go into the kitchen and turn the lights off. Turn all the lights off. Only the TV flickering and lighting up the ceiling above the bed. Turn the sound off and light a cigarette.

She comes out of the loo and stands in front of me and smiles. I smile back and she takes off her tight scruffy jeans and asks if I'm not going to turn the TV off and I say I'd rather have it on. She takes off her vest and smiles at me again and she really does have great breasts. A new video starts and I don't know what band it is but the blue light is playing over her legs. It's probably only the light from the TV but her body looks very tanned. We lie down in bed and kiss. She has her arms around me and I let my hand slide down her back. We're on our side and she moves her leg on top of mine and I press against her. I kiss her neck and I have a hard on. Her hand finds her way down to my underpants and I try to remember what colour they are. One hand on her hip and I let it move along the top of her knickers and down her butt. She grabs my cock and I kiss her cheek and hear the sirens from an ambulance outside. My hand moves back to her hip whilst she slowly jerks me off. I moan quietly in her ear and start pulling her knickers down a bit. One finger inside her and she's wet. I finger her for a while and then fall down on my back. She stops jerking me off and takes my hand and places it between her legs again. My finger inside her again. A strong pale light on my arm. She breathers faster and faster and when I think she's coming she moves my hand away and looks at me and smiles. She starts jerking me off again then sits on top of me and pushes my cock inside her. The sirens are back and I wonder if it's the same one as before and if someone is dead or just hurt. She leans forward and kisses my chest and starts riding me. It's insanely good and the pale light shines like a spotlight from the side and she's faster and faster. She leans forward again and says, you don't have to worry, you can come inside me. I nod and groan loudly when she rotates with her whole body.

The pale light disappears and she starts riding me again. Hard and fast. I get dizzy for a few seconds and it feels like I'm going to be sick but it passes quickly. She groans louder and louder. I hear her whisper oh my god and she screams when she comes. She smiles and continues to ride me harder and harder and faster and the light is very pale when I come inside her.

It's sunny outside. I stare at the back yard. The trees nearly reach my window and move in that really strange way again. The thin branches and their leaves wave slowly and lifelessly. Somehow they remind me of lifeless human arms. Dead human arms. Dead humans hung upside down with their arms free in the wind. I go outside with a rubbish bag and when I come back I sit down and light a cigarette.

I often think of stories and unusual facts that I've heard somewhere. Many stories are completely pointless and it sometimes irritates me so much that I use up my memory so pointlessly. On the other hand, what are important memories? It doesn't really matter, just as long as you remember something.

Micke's answering machine says he's at the pool hall in Kungsholmen and I think: which one?

Take the 54 and get off across the street from the pool hall where I used to play computer games when I was at school. I pass the kebab shop next door and realise I need to eat something. The actual pool rooms are supposed to be massive but I've never been in there. Instead I go straight up to where the computer games are, which is where Micke should be. He's sitting on a bar stool in the far corner and I can see the light flickering across his face. A boy in a baseball cap who's maybe twelve-thirteen stands behind him, watching. He's holding a packet of cigarettes and seems to be squeezing it. I go and stand beside him. I vaguely remember this game. Seem to remember I played it once about a year ago when I was drunk and we had gone to some all-night arcade.

'Hey, what's up?' I say

'Oh hi… well, yeah.'

I can feel the young boy in the baseball cap who's clutching the cigarettes staring at me. I watch the game and this He-Man lookalike in it. He's wearing a grey loincloth, and holding a shield and a chain mace. You're supposed to go through caves and mountains and alleyways and secret chambers. Sometimes wizards appear who throw poisonous crystal balls and sometimes snakes or other creatures writhe and they can deliver an electric shock so you lose energy. Or you could just be killed. If you manage to murder a wizard or cut some other creature's throat the creature will be transformed into a coin which says five, ten or fifty. You're supposed to pick up the coins and when you've moved through a cave (or mountain or whatever it is) the sum of all the coins you've collected appears on the screen together with a list of all your weapons. Twenty dollars will swap your chain mace for a crossbow. If you have a lot of money you can get different types of anti-vulnerability shields or more energy or some kind of laser machine gun.

'Fuck, check how far he's got!' says the friend of the boy in the baseball cap who's now stood behind us.

'Mmm,' the baseball cap boy replies without looking at his friend, who's wearing undone basketball shoes and a Walkman in the pocket of his hoodie.

'FUCK FUCKING COCKSUCKING GAME,' Micke suddenly screams. First he punches the screen with his fist, then he stands up and shakes the whole machine and finishes off by sitting down on the stool banging his head against the screen. He stands up and says fuck quietly and looks at me and smiles.

'But what the fuck, you got to the cave people and the laser spiders,' the boy with the baseball cap says and stares at Micke.

'Yeah which you probably never will,' he grins back and lights a cigarette.

'Shut it,' the baseball cap boy says.

'Fucking queer!' the boy in the basketball shoes screams behind us as we start walking towards the exit. I'm thinking that I never dared being that cocky with older guys when I was twelve.

'How about a kebab?' Micke asks and looks at me.

'I was just thinking the same thing when I arrived,' I say and look at his forehead, wet with sweat.

'A kebab,' Micke says to the Turk.

'Begosmal?'

'What?'

'Beg?'

'Yes please.'

'Hot sauce?'

'Yes.'

'I'll have one too,' I say and put the right change on the counter. We don't say a word while we're eating. Micke eats his pickled chillies whole. Even the stalk or whatever it's called.

I wipe my mouth with a napkin from a burger stall and look at Micke as he lights a cigarette.

'How did you get here anyway?' He exhales smoke.

'I don't know.'

He runs his hand through his hair. We're quiet for thirty seconds or so and he looks out at S:t Eriksgatan with one of those empty stares he sometimes has.

'No, what does one know really?' He grins feebly. We're quiet again.

He starts drumming his hands against his knees and says finally:

'Nothing.' He smiles faintly and continues to stare out the window with his absent look and the boy with the baseball cap is standing on the pavement outside doing karate kicks in the air at his friend.

It's half past nine. First thing I do when I wake up is to call in sick. Shower and find a pair of cotton trousers I've probably not worn since last summer. Drink a glass of juice and eat a couple of sandwiches filled with those fit-for-life bean sprouts. Sit by the window and look down on everyone going into Metro. Mostly pensioners.

Just as I'm about to call Micke and I'm halfway through dialling his number I remember that he was filling in for someone at the bar in Vickan today. I go back to the window and open it. Sit down on the window sill and stare at the clouds which look like atom bombs. I don't know, but when I hear the words atom bomb I always think of that black and white mushroom cloud photo in the school books. I guess it's a childhood memory, thinking that the atom bomb didn't seem particularly frightening. It's somehow stuck and every time I think about the clouds in the sky I always think about atom bombs. And the Japanese?

When I was a child I was convinced you could walk on the clouds. That they were like giant cotton wool balls. Or deep snow. I often thought of it and it wasn't until I was thirteen fourteen that it was completely clear to me that you couldn't even touch a cloud.

When the whole family flew somewhere and we went through a cloud and it got foggy I never asked my parents why or how we could travel through the clouds just like that. I remember I didn't want to seem like a fool by asking something so stupid. Thought that it was simply because the plane travelled so fast and with such force and that's why we made it through.

Another thing I remember thinking about when we were on a plane was that the plane would be blown to pieces and all the passengers would be thrown out into the air. I remember hoping I would be saved by landing on a cloud. This situation that I put myself in every time we flew somewhere always ended with me dying as there was nothing to eat on this cloud. I remember I might have jumped over to other passing clouds but there was nothing to eat there either. I died from starvation, lying deep inside a cloud or unless I decided to jump to earth and died by hitting the ground.

It really annoys me when I remember lots of pointless things from my childhood. It happens more and more regularly and there is no point and the only thing it does is annoy me.

I close the window and put a t-shirt on and go down to Metro. There is a new type of light beer, Spendrups Extra Dry, and I buy five and a litre of juice. The blonde girl who's worked here for a month or so is at the till and I think to myself how hard it is to work out the ages of the girls working at the supermarket. Fourteen? Eighteen? Twenty? Sixteen-seventeen I think. Either way I think that I would like to fuck this girl and that when I've received my change and she's said thank you, I simply say: "Hey, by the way, would you like to come up to mine and fuck for a little bit?" and that she simply answers something like: "Sure, let me just serve this next customer first."

I put the beer in the fridge and then head down to the video shop and rent a porn film.

The film starts with a girl lying on a bed in a hotel room looking bored and staring out the window. After a little while she starts unbuttoning her shirt and touching her breasts. When she's done that for a bit she stands up and takes her skirt and knickers off and lies back down on the bed. One hand touches one of her nipples whilst the other slowly slides down between her legs. When she's masturbated and groaned loudly for a few minutes a bellboy enters the room with a stack of towels. When he sees her lying there he drops the towels and she spreads her legs open even more. The camera zooms in on her very wet pussy. She screams: "Oh please, come and fuck me!" The bellboy slowly moves towards the bed. She groans: "I need a cock" and sits up and unbuttons the bellboy's trousers and starts sucking his half-erect cock.

When she's finished sucking his cock and he's come in her face and she's smeared the come over her tits I rewind and play that "Oh please come and fuck me!" and "I need a cock" four or five times.

In the evening they call from Hard Rock Café and ask if I can work tomorrow and I say yes, I suppose I can. The girl who does the rotas (and who is pretty) says good... we'll expect you tomorrow.

When I pass Odenplan on my way back from work I bump into Magnus, an old friend from school days.

We never normally see each other anymore but occasionally we'll bump into each other in the street.

I ask him what he's doing and he says he's at stage school. He says a lot of embarrassing things like "acting has become a drug" and that he's "found himself".

I remember when we were in year ten. I think it was year ten and it was spring. Magnus, Lasse and I had bought hash from a boy from another class. He was known as the dopehead in school and we had talked for months about buying a gram from him.

I remember we got the piece of hash during a lunch break and Lasse hid it in his pencil case. We decided to meet in Observatorielunden that evening.

I think Bob Marley had recently died. Either way it was cool to listen to him and Magnus had brought a cassette player on which he played "I Shot the Sheriff" on repeat.

Lasse had bought tobacco and I had bought a corn pipe and Magnus said he knew what to do so we let him pack the pipe. We lit up and the pipe did the rounds and I remember my hands shaking when it was my first turn. Magnus demonstrated how Bob Marley had smoked in some video and we tried to smoke just like him. After a while I felt sick and Lasse felt sick but Magnus danced around the cassette player blasting out "I Shot the Sheriff".

The next day we kept telling everyone we had been high as kites even though we suspected that Magnus had only acted. The whole week we talked about getting another gram.

I guess it was about two weeks after we had smoked hash that I came home from school one afternoon to a completely quiet flat. Mum and dad who had just got married again were sat at the kitchen table in silence, staring at me when I said hi. I vividly remember that moment when I sat down at the table and felt there was a strange atmosphere. It was mum who first said something, she said: "The school counsellor called today" and I said: "So what?" Then my dad took over and said, threateningly: "What are you up to?" We had a fight that I remember in detail but don't want to.

I went into my room and cried. I couldn't stop crying. My mum's words in my ear over and over again "Are you going to become a junkie?" I cried a long time.

Half seven I meet Tobbe at the cinema. We watch a new film with John Cleese which is moderately funny. When I get back home I get angry with myself for forgetting the title of the film. Contemplate looking in the paper but change my mind.

Wake up around midday and realise it was only a dream. Try to remember: I went ashore on this island. It was a sunny - perhaps Greek? - island. The mermaid appeared when I crossed the bridge. Naturally she was blonde and somehow her fins disappeared when I talked to her. She was incredibly, almost horrifyingly, beautiful. Happy, curious and innocent (?) and I fell head over heels. For some reason she left the sea for me. I was given some kind of exclusive right to her but I was constantly worried that someone else would discover her. I was her sole living contact and I told her about how to live on land… and then the emptiness when you wake up.

I never usually suffer from Monday morning depression.

Get woken up at nine by a jolly Hard Rock voice that wants me to work. "All is one, you know..." and "sometimes you have to put yourself out a little". No point trying to wriggle out of it.

Get down to Hard Rock around ten and start preparing the salad buffet.

We open at eleven and the only good song that plays on the cassette player all day is "Sledgehammer." Three hours of constant stress and that awful slimy character with combed back waxed hair and a deep tan sitting at one of my tables. That type that for some reason wants to know the waiters. Who calls waiters and bar staff by their name. I make sure I smile as painfully and artificially as I can when he says well hello Johan, what's up? and continues with:

'Were you at Melody last night?' I say no.

'It was absolutely buzzing,' he says and everything feels very awkward.

Half two I close my station and go home. Manage to get about half an hour's sleep before Tobbe calls and asks if I want to get absolutely plastered.

Half an hour later Tobbe is at mine in some new chic shirt. He's wearing shades when he opens the first of our five Green Pearl.

Head over to Micke's around one. We listen to old Ramones records (Rock'n'Roll Radio… Let's go) and Micke hands me a cold light beer and we sit down on his balcony. It feels like the first day of summer. The traffic in Hornsgatan is at boiling point and we both light a cigarette and just feel the heat, Ramones and the beer.

It must be about three when Tobbe turns up. He immediately sits down by the phone and calls someone who seems to be called John.

Micke is taking a shower and I sit in a big grey leather chair and play with my packet of Marlboro. Suddenly Tobbe puts his hand over the receiver and asks if I want to buy some coke.

'How much does he want?'

'600… and it's good stuff, I've bought from him before,' he says in a low voice.

'Ok,' I say and shrug my shoulders.

He starts talking to this John again and says I'll take three grams then. And then: 'In about an hour.'

Micke comes out of the shower dressed in a pair of trendy shorts and is wearing shades. He puts some cream on and does macho poses in front of us and we laugh feebly.

Tobbe asks if we should have some tonight and I say are you not working and he smiles and says he swapped shifts with Anders.

'You can have the coke back that I owe you,' he says to Micke who moves his shades to the top of his head and says that's cool.

Tobbe gets a cassette out with the new Bowie album on and puts it in the stereo and turns the volume up. The song seems to be called Videocrime.

I'm the only one out of all of us who has a car and around half four we all go to this John who neither Micke or I have met.

After some time we've found Skeppargatan. There don't seem to be any apartments in this block that cost less than a million.

Tobbe tells us to wait in the car for now.

After five minutes he returns. We decide to go to Hamngatan Ett for a beer. On our way there Tobbe tells us that a really hot girl opened the door at John's. She was only wearing knickers and he says he nearly got a hard on and we laugh and say he's lying and he says no, I promise.

After the beers I drive Micke and Tobbe back and go home to have a shower. My dad's left a message on the answering machine saying why don't you get in touch occasionally and I think well I do sometimes. I went out for dinner with him like a week ago. Have a shower and listen to a load of awful music videos on MTV whilst I get ready. It's seven by the time I get down to Big Burger to eat. Order two Biggers but only eat one of them. For some reason I feel stressed. I try to calm myself down by reading an Expressen that someone's left behind. Smoke a couple of cigarettes then take the tube to Micke's.

Tobbe is already there when I arrive. He pours me a glass of Codorníu and I stare at the envelope on the table. Micke calls a girl and Tobbe puts on a porn film called Hot Flesh. Micke signs to us to lower the volume.

Wake up around two and feel awful. My nose is completely blocked and the radio's playing "R-O-C-K." I get up and stumble over to the loo and try to blow my nose. Nothing but blood. My head hurts and the chorus to "Paradise City" pierces my head. "Take me down to the Paradise city where the grass is green and the girls are pretty". Mats who was in my class in high school and is now studying law calls after I've blown blood out of my nose for the fourth time. We decide to meet up at Yo-Yo at three.

I get on the 47 at Dalagatan and it's hellishly hot on the bus and my headache is killing me. At Norra Bantorget some guy gets on who's maybe twenty-five-thirty and seems completely out of it. At first I think he's OD'd when he stands there with a vacant look in his eyes. He grunts and the shades have slid down his nose. Completely on purpose he hits his head against the handrail. I can hear how much it hurts but he doesn't seem to mind. Wondering if he's mental or something like that. A lady asks him if he's got asthma and he slurs something unintelligible. She asks if he wants an inhaler and he nods. It turns out he doesn't know how to use it and the heat is unbearable and I hope the nutter is getting off soon. He stumbles off at NK and I get off at Norrmalmstorg.

We're sitting outside and Mats tells me about a gay guy in his class who comes on to him sometimes.

'It's fucked up, he says a few times and grins a little and touches his shades.

He drinks his beer quickly and we have nothing to talk about and I feel the headache disappearing. I tell him I was out last night. That everything was as it always is at Melody. That I saw his (ex?) girlfriend with some advertising guy. That some shitty band played. That the bouncers threw Viktor out. That he should have been there.

He says I should have been there at the last Asgasquen. That I would have liked it. That he's fucked five economics girls in the last month. That he has an exam soon. I glance at his book about sentencing and procedural law lying on the table.

My beer is finished and my head feels heavy and good. Mats leans forward and asks if I can get two grams of coke for next weekend. I say maybe and he says that would be ace and I say call me in a few days.

A few minutes of silence whilst we both smoke a cigarette.

'I should probably head back home... working tonight and that,' I finally say and put the cigarette packet in my pocket.

'Mmm, yeah, well I should be studying.' We get up.

Things are like they always are at work when you're on the day shift. I get down there for half nine and I'm the only waiting staff who's arrived. The cleaners have just finished and are drinking coffee and smoking. I pour myself a coffee and sit at the counter opposite the kitchen and say hello to Nicke who's sitting on a bench next to the grill in the kitchen reading DN.

When I've finished my coffee and smoked a cigarette Helene and another waitress called Viktoria arrive. We say hello and Helene says what she always says, that she's tired and then reels off a list of places she's been the night before. She dissolves four caffeine tablets in a glass of water which she takes with her when we go over to our stations at the far end of the restaurant. We start taking the chairs down off the tables.

Five past ten Fredrik arrives and gets told off by Mattias (today's shift manager) because he's late and Fredrik says something about some bus and then yells over to me where I'm standing at a table at the back of the shop:

'Hey Johan... look, I'll start with the salad bar straight away.'

I nod and Helene yells back:

'Fantastic.'

Fredrik pulls a face and heads over to the kitchen.

Twenty-five past ten when we're done with all the prep Patrik arrives. Mattias and Helene and Viktoria and I are at the counter serving ourselves breakfast and Mattias says fucking decent of you to fill in just after Patrik has said how knackered he is. There's a few seconds silence and I continue to slice some cheese to put on my toast.

'Mattias...' Helene looks pleadingly in a slightly humorous way at him. 'You have to try and get someone else... otherwise we're understaffed for the third day in a row.'

'Mmm, yeah I know... I'm going to try Tobbe and...' Mattias goes off to make a call and Patrik goes into the kitchen to help Fredrik with the salad bar and the rest of us head upstairs and sit down at the round table and start eating.

After a few minutes we can hear the salad bar being wheeled out and after another minute Fredrik and Patrik come upstairs and sit down with a beer glass of coffee each.

'Ok, three minutes to go,' says Mattias and gets up. He sounds as if he was talking to a band who was just about to go on stage.

At eleven the lights go off and on where we're seated and the music is turned on and the first song is "Listen To Your Heart" by Roxette and we stub our cigarettes out and watch Mattias unlock the door.

It's been ages since there was one of those mental parties but when I get to Tom's three bedroom flat in Linnégatan I feel calm and like this could turn into a really great party. It's only four in the afternoon but most people seem to be here already (?). The usual and loads of others. Tom greets me by singing the chorus to "Why Can't This Be Love" by Van Halen and he seems high. I check the living room and Louise and Nettan are lying on the extremely low leather sofa drinking fizzy wine straight out of the bottle. Viktor and Tobbe are sitting on the floor by the stereo rummaging through the record collection. Marie's on the window sill with some guy I've never seen before. Linda is talking with Robert who works at Collage and two other guys that I recognise but whose names I can't recall. A pretty girl in a mini skirt is sitting on top of a table talking on the phone and smoking a joint. I'm wondering if I should call Mats.

Tom introduces me to a couple of girls that I recognise from Dailys and they turn out to be Tina and Mimi. He asks if I want champagne and hands me a bottle of fizzy wine. I open it and when the cork hits the ceiling with a bang Viktor turns around and says hello and I say hello as I lift the bottle to my mouth. Just as I'm lighting a cigarette a champagne cork lands on my head and I turn around and Micke is laughing out loud and asks how things are and I say fine and he asks me if I have any coke and I say no and he says maybe you want some of mine then. He turns to Tom and smiles and asks if he has a free mirror and Tom laughs and says sure. Jocke enters the room and asks me how things are and I say splendid and watch Tom as he grabs the girl on the table who's still on the phone. He stands her up and starts looking for a mirror amongst the ashtrays and bottles. I notice that both the TV sets are on but no one is watching. One of them is showing some music video and the other a black and white film. Tom hands Micke the mirror and he chops up some lines and one of the girls (Tina?) rolls up a tenner and Micke hands her the mirror and she snorts a line.

When everybody's had one I go into the kitchen to get a glass of champagne and there are some guys and a girl by the kitchen table giggling and having some lines. We say hello to each other and I grab a glass and go into another room. There are some people there I don't know drinking wine. Two guys are in an armchair cuddling each other but stop when I look at them.

I go back to Tom and the others. Viktor's just had another line and I ask Tom how long they've been going.

'How long? We've only just started,' he says and grins. 'No but seriously, since about one, more people will probably turn up later.'

'For sure,' I say.

The telephone is finally free and I call Mats but the music is too loud and I can't hear what he says. I swap telephones and just as I pick up the receiver a new gang arrives that I say hello to. Tom is in the hallway hugging one of the girls and I give the address to Mats and say he can pop by if he feels like it.

When I get back to the living room Micke is holding an old Ramones record and looks happy.

'Hey, leave that one for a while,' Viktor shouts at him and manages to make himself heard over Blue Monday.

'Fucking hell, that really pisses me off, are you some kind of almighty DJ or what?' Micke shouts back.

Tobbe and the girl in the mini skirt are in the same armchair and try to snort the leftovers of a few lines. I grab a glass of champagne and sit down in an empty armchair. There's a lot of people now and Micke pushes his way towards me and sits down on the armrest and smiles.

'How good is this?'

'Mmm,' I say. 'What's the time?'

'Who gives a shit what time it is?'

'Do you know what time it is?'

'No.'

A girl in black leggings approaches us and asks Micke if he's got any coke and Micke says ask Tom.

I see Robert and Linda standing in a corner and he's got one hand inside her jumper and she just looks high and bored. Tom comes up to us and squats down in front of us and has a drag of his joint and says there aren't enough chicks here.

'Yeah, how about you sort that out then,' says Micke and smiles.

'I guess I could put some effort in,' he smiles back.

I go to the loo and when I get back the girl in leggings is looking at me.

'Don't you work at Hard Rock?'

'Yeah.'

'I remember you, you served us last week. Don't you recognise me?'

'No... I don't know, maybe.' Incredibly stupid question.

'Come!' she says and takes my hand and we go back in the loo again. She locks the door and smiles at me and I'm wondering how old she is, seventeen, eighteen? I check her body out and she's wearing a tight white polo neck and she notices I'm fixating on her breasts. She giggles and takes a step closer towards me and I grab her firm butt and she giggles again and we kiss. She presses up against me and I have a hard on and one of my hands slides down her back under her jumper and suddenly she lets go of me and steps back a couple of paces and pulls her jumper off and looks at me.

'Do you like this?' She giggles.

I don't know why, but I smile nervously and stare at her perfect breasts.

'I want to do it here on the floor,' she says and starts pulling her leggings off. She is high as a kite.

I slowly start unbuttoning my trousers. She takes her knickers off and lies down on the cold white bathroom floor and spreads her legs. I stare at her body and she sits up on her knees and starts sucking my cock. Somebody bangs on the door and I hear Micke shouting, Johan are you in there? She sucks hard and when I start groaning loudly she stops and lies back down on the floor. Her tanned body in strange contrast to the cold white tiles and she gasps when I enter her.

When we come out of the loo a guy grabs the door and says about fucking time. The girl in the leggings gives me a kiss and says see you later and goes into the kitchen. Tobbe comes up to me and asks if she was any good and I shrug my shoulders and he asks if I want pizza and I say get me a Cacciatora and think that it's going to be a long night and I should probably have another line.

It's six o'clock and Sunday when I wake up and I quickly work out that I must have slept for fifteen hours. Have a quick shower and go downstairs to Seven Eleven. Buy a couple of sandwiches and a diet Coke and head over to Vasaparken and sit down on the grass. The sky is clear and it looks like it's going to be a hellishly hot day. I hoover up the sandwiches and open the can of coke and light a cigarette and lie on my back and close my eyes thinking that I should be doing something on a day like this.

When I've smoked two cigarettes a drunk appears and sits down on a bench a few metres away. He keeps staring at me and it's becoming irritating after a while so I head home.

Ten past eight I call Tobbe and he says he's been wide awake since five. We agree that we should go over to Djurgårdsbrunn and that we have to get some more people to come. I call Micke and his answering machine is on and when it starts recording I shout pick up pick up wake up and eventually he does. After a few minutes he's awake enough to be able to speak properly and I say I'm heading over to his in a bit.

At half nine I'm in Linda's car and feel the wind through my hair. It's one of those convertible sports cars that look as if it's straight from a sixties Bond movie and it really is summer when we cross S:t Eriksbron.

When we've picked up Tobbe and Micke and are in a traffic jam on Strandvägen, Micke gets out his caffeine tin for the second time.

'Just a few too many Valium last night,' he says and grins feebly.

'If you hadn't taken them you wouldn't have come down yet. You wouldn't have gone to fucking sleep until next week some time,' says Tobbe.

Linda turns the radio on and they say… 'and now a classic from 1982' and Per Gessle sings "summer days hey hey summer days lips on lips two hearts on fire", and Linda sings along.

When we arrive at Djurgårdsbrunn Inn they're just about to open and Linda runs up to give a waitress a hug, she seems to be called Mia, and Micke says hello to the barman. There's probably not a single barman he doesn't know.

Tobbe and I take a seat at the bar and Linda comes up to us and we sit down in the sun. She lights a cigarette and asks Tobbe if he'll be drinking and he says no and she says good, then you can drive the car back to town and he says sure.

Micke sits down with us and takes off his shades.

'Does anyone remember Freddy being at the party last night?' he asks and smiles and we shake our heads and are only moderately interested.

'He was.'

'Can you buy me some wine?' Linda asks and looks at him.

'What do you want then?'

'Half a bottle of white… anything… and a bowl of ice and lemon.'

'Sure, anyone else want anything? We're not officially open yet but we'll make an exception for you.'

No one laughs and Micke puts his shades back on and pushes them up over his forehead and asks what do you want then?

'Pepsi,' Tobbe says.

'Sparkling water with ice,' I say.

The heat is unbearable and when Linda has finished her wine we decide to go down to the canal to lie down in the shade. On the way we stop at the ice cream van and Linda insists on having chocolate sauce on her ice cream even though the vendor says you can only have it with soft ice. She finally gets her way and the rest of us are happy with a plain soft ice.

When we're laid on the grass Linda starts complaining about her ice cream.

'She told you not to get chocolate sauce,' Micke says.

'So what, this is not chocolate sauce, this is chocolate topping.'

'Big difference.'

'It's fucking disgusting,' she says and throws her ice cream cone in the canal.

Some ducks are approaching and I break my cone up and feed them. One duck is less than half a metre away and I like watching it chew. I'm wondering if I would be able to catch it or if it would bite my fingers off.

It slowly waddles away from me.

My parents still live in the same apartment we lived in before I left home. It's a pretty large four bedroom flat halfway up Rörstransgatan and even though it's only one stop away on the tube it feels like I've travelled very far every time I enter the hallway.

It's six o'clock when I ring the doorbell and my mum opens the door and I'm in that hallway again.

I'm not at all dissatisfied with growing up here but every time I come here, go into the living room, go over to the window and look out at Solna far in the distance, a strange sense of hopelessness comes over me. I've no idea why, but I always feel a bit low and a bit scared when I sit down in the old rococo furniture. I always try to hide my melancholy and I do so now too when we're sitting here talking and drinking coffee and my mum's Gula Blend packet is on the table and she talks about some new musical score and I pretend to be interested.

When she goes into the kitchen to get something I'm thinking that I probably had a happy childhood. Harmonious. I'm thinking that it should be nice to come back to your childhood home. At least I'm relieved that Eric Satie is not playing. It makes me so incredibly depressed even if it is quite beautiful I guess.

I stay for an hour or so and before I leave we make plans to go out for dinner one night.

Come home around eight and feel like doing something. Head over to Micke's and we have a beer each but he's a bit sluggish and doesn't want to do anything and after half an hour I go home again. As I stop by the red lights in Fridhemsplan it starts raining. I buy a take away pizza and a Svenska Dagbladet and when I've finished my pizza and read the newspaper for a bit Micke calls and says he's perked up and wants to do something.

We meet up at Peppar around half eleven and he drinks Stella but I've started feeling a bit sick and order a sparkling water. Around half one he suggests going to Caféet but I say I want to go home and he says he's going anyway to check out if anyone he knows is there. When I've finished my third Ramlösa and Micke his third Stella we leave and walk up Odengatan. It's spitting a bit and Micke curses the lack of cabs. We part by the corner of Västmannagatan where I take a left and he a right.

The big news when I arrive at Hard Rock is that Electric Boys have trashed a hotel room somewhere in Härjedalen.

'Get this,' says Helene, who frequently fucks them. 'They've thrown a TV out, and a door from the second floor.' She sounds as if she's the one being charged.

'And broken into the store room and taken forty beers, fuck me that's rock'n'roll,' Micke grins.

We're having coffee and decide to go out later when we finish and five to six I go downstairs to change. When I get back up we start talking about how many guests are tourists now.

'Fat Americans… sometimes they tip you loads and sometimes nothing,' says Micke.

'Their tour guide has probably told them that they don't have to tip in Sweden,' says Helene whilst idly flicking through Expressen.

'Mmm,' I say and look at Jonas who's the shift manager tonight. He's chatting to Erik and I'm pretty sure it's about some drug deal.

We're in Viktor's two bedroom flat in Engelbrektsgatan and the balcony door is open and the white curtain flutters like a ghost. It looks like a film.

I'm half lying on a brown leather chair and feel a bit knackered. Fredrik and Tobbe are standing by Viktor's synthesizer which is connected to the stereo. They're giggling and playing with the worst sounds (Jetwars, Devildoom, Zombielaugh etc) and it's not the ideal morning after music. It's not technically a morning after for me. We only had a few beers at Pipeline after work yesterday and I'm probably only tired because of the lack of sleep.

'Listen! Cavescream!' says Fredrik and turns around and grimaces along with the horrendous scream sound.

Viktor is shouting from the kitchen, food is ready and we get in there and inspect the potato dauphinoise and beef patties suspiciously. I don't know why but Viktor enjoys cooking different things.

Eva and Nettan who are seated at the table get up, plates ready. Tobbe gets out a Coteaux du Languedoc and starts looking for a corkscrew.

'I don't know if I've got enough cutlery to go around,' Viktor says.

'Well that's bloody great, thinking of that now,' Eva smiles.

When we've finished eating Viktor puts on Elvis Costello's latest and Eva sighs and says what rubbish.

'Anyone got any coke?' Tobbe asks.

'Just over a gram, but it's pure as fuck,' Viktor says and goes into the hallway to fetch it.

He comes back and Eva chops out a small line and snorts it in one and says Jesus, that's strong. She holds her hand over her nose and Tobbe chops out a fat one for himself and Viktor shakes his head and says:

'I wouldn't do that if I were you.'

'What the fuck, I want a kick,' he replies and starts on the line. When he's snorted less than half of it he looks up at Eva and me teary-eyed for a few seconds. 'Yeah, it's pretty strong,' he says quietly and then the blood starts gushing out of his nose.

'God this shit is so disgusting,' Eva says.

Viktor goes off to get some paper.

When Tobbe's recovered we go back into the living room and sit down and Eva walks up to the stereo and turns off Elvis Costello and puts on Fine Young Cannibals. It's nine o'clock but no one seems particularly geared up to do anything, apart from Tobbe.

So my mother calls me when I get back from work and suggests a family dinner on Sunday. Of course I say, that sounds nice and when I've hung up I go and stand in front of the mirror. If I go to the tanning salon tomorrow and Saturday I'll probably look fresher on Sunday. Not that I should care, but.

I usually get my coke off Tom. He usually buys it from Niels and this Niels who looks like a stock broker and is maybe twenty-five is having lunch at Hard Rock with some friends and I serve them and even though Tom has introduced me to him once he doesn't recognise me. Everyone orders the vegetarian platter apart from one of them who wants a sirloin steak.

As I wait for the food in the kitchen I remember a story Tom once told me. He'd heard it from Niels. Apparently some South Americans smuggling coke into Europe kidnap infants and remove all the intestines and organs and things and stuff them full of cocaine. Once they're on the plane they sit with their sleeping baby all wrapped up in a blanket and no one suspects anything.

When I get home I turn the stereo on and listen to Elvis Costello. He sings "I wish you had known me when I was alive" and it just sounds depressing so I turn it off and watch some music videos instead and then head down to the tanning salon.

The girl at the till is blonde and suntanned and has a perfect body and she smiles and looks horny and when I've been tanning for a while and start to sweat I get a hard on when I think about her body.

In the evening Fredrik and I go to Melody. We get incredibly drunk and high and lose each other after a bit. Everything's spinning and I'm giggling almost continuously. Talk to lots of people I know but have no real clue what I'm saying.

At the afterparty at this girl's house they only play Imperiet and Electric Boys and I'm on a sofa starting to come down and feel sick. Get given some Valium by someone I don't know. A girl next to me is completely ashen and makes regular trips to the bathroom to throw up. Sandra tells me the ashen girl feels rough because she's on penicillin and has had too much tequila and smoked too much hash and taken too many Sobril for some reason. (Because her boyfriend slept with someone else on the same day they had their first anniversary? I don't know, can't concentrate on what she's saying.)

The singer from Baltimore (I don't know, maybe it just looks like him), is on the floor together with two girls who have perfect faces. I think they're smoking a joint.

I would have really liked to have seen her in daylight. What part of town? What time? Where is she? I'm asking myself these pathetic morning after questions whilst lying in an empty bed with a pink teddy bear next to me. In the shower I turn my head up towards the water and remember I met this peroxide blonde who hangs out with Electric Boys. You hardly meet anyone who doesn't. It seems everyone's fucking or knows someone in that band. Anyway, the blonde introduced me to Sandra and I gave Sandra and the groupie Lena some coke.

I remember Melody was rammed and it was a promo gig for Toni Holgersson and Peter LeMarc I think.

We went to an afterparty at someone's flat in Östermalm and then we got a cab back here.

When I get home I sit down at the kitchen table which is piled high with pizza boxes. Eat two grapefruits and feel good. I've run out of cigarettes so I quickly change into clean clothes and go out to get some more. Call Linda from the phone booth in Odenplan and we meet up at half three at Matpalatset. She's wearing a white vest that finishes above her belly button. We drink café au lait and I wait for her to tell me something about her latest shags.

She usually does and it usually really turns me on. Realise it was ages since we last fucked.

Instead she starts telling me about her relationship with some bouncer. It's clear she thinks I'm going to react badly. Break down or press the knife against my artery and I'm thinking cut it out, you wouldn't care if I was the one in a relationship? I don't know, maybe I should care, but I don't.

Orup's latest is blasting out of the speaker and I try and push her for more details to see if maybe I will react at all. She waxes lyrical about everything and really gets going and gives off an impression of being "deeeep in love" and I feel nothing. I actually think she's acting. She really wants to be in love.

I feel like saying something like "we've never been more than fuck friends – so why worry?" but I keep quiet and let her rabbit on about how this bouncer's (is he called Anders?) flat is decorated and she makes sure every other sentence is scattered with bits like "I never thought I would fall in love with a bouncer" or "really, he is studying to be an accountant".

We go for a walk downtown and in Kungsgatan we bump into her bouncer of course.

I take the tube home and call Tobbe.

We meet up at Tranan around seven and drink uninhibitedly until five to midnight when we go to Big Burger and order a Bigger each with all the extras.

We part by the underground entrance and I walk home and there's an acid house documentary on cable that I watch until I fall asleep.

'I'm beginning to fucking hate all kids,' Helene says when she barges into the coffee room and opens the helium cannister and starts blowing up balloons.

I finish my water and get up and go into the kitchen to collect two Kidburgers and a Where's the beef sandwich. It's Saturday and it's two in the afternoon and almost all the guests are families with kids. On my way to table eleven I see Fia cleaning up spilt ice cream from a table. Martin, who's a kind of play leader at these so called "Familyrock" Saturdays, is lifting some kids up onto a gigantic stuffed toy cow, set up in the middle of the restaurant.

'Would you also like to ride the cow Henry?' I hear him say to some kid when I walk past. I serve table eleven and just as I've said enjoy your lunch, the mother says to the two children:

'If you ask nicely you might get a balloon each.'

'Mmm, sure I can arrange that,' I say and try to smile and feel stressed when I leave.

I know the food for table two is already waiting in the serving hatch. Go back into the coffee room and Helene is still there tying strings to the balloons.

'It's fucking outrageous, some kid's birthday and he wants ten balloons. I don't know why we agree to it.'

I'm inflating my two balloons when Fredrik bursts in and stands in front of the mirror and runs his hand through his hair. His forehead is gleaming with sweat and he stares at himself for a long time.

'Fucking hell,' he says quietly and gets a packet of cigarettes out and when he's lit up he turns towards me and Helene leaves with her bunch of balloons and Fredrik says:

'Give me drunk hard-rockers pouring beers over each other any day.'

'You can have my evening shift,' says David who enters with an Expressen and a cheeseburger. 'I'm working between three and two.' He sits down at the small rickety table.

Neither Fredrik nor I say anything and I tie the last string to a pink balloon. Fredrik goes up to the table and takes a couple of hard drags and puts the cigarette out and says calmly: 'I don't give a flying fuck,' and leaves.

I grab my two balloons and go into the kitchen and burn myself on a plate that's most probably been under the heater fifteen minutes.

Decide to deliver the balloons first.

Around four a gang of hard-rockers who are likely from out of town arrive and look completely bewildered when there's screaming kids everywhere. They've probably heard from someone that Hard Rock is where it's at, it's always full of rockers.

Around half five things begin to calm down and I see a busboy, who I think is called Per, help Martin wheel back the ice cream stand that's been out all day under the hologram picture.

I go and stand by the kitchen ticket machine and count food vouchers and credit card slips. Micke comes in wearing his leather jacket and slaps my back and I lose count and say hi.

'So how was today?'

'What do you think?'

'Hey, the heavy metal shift is not particularly exciting either.' He goes up to the bar and pours himself a light beer and gets a staff food ticket and goes downstairs again and leaves his beer on the counter and hands the food ticket to a guy in the kitchen and says something to him and the guy in the kitchen throws a few fries at him.

Quarter past six I clock out and hand a staff food ticket to the kitchen and go downstairs to change.

When I get back upstairs again my barbecue burger is ready and I sit down at the counter and start eating. Carina comes up and asks what I'm doing tonight.

'Sleeping,' I say with a mouth full of food.

'You're not going to Melody then?'

'No.'

I don't understand how she does it, she must be at Melody four-five days a week, regardless of whether she works from nine in the morning until midnight, she always gets a cab there.

Micke is at the kitchen ticket machine talking to Fredrik who's putting an order through and doesn't seem to understand what he's saying.

'… and the bitter fight against the dreaded heavy metal army has started… around two we will have made their troops retreat.' He does some shadowboxing.

When I've finished eating I say bye to Micke and Fredrik and a girl in the shop whose name I've forgotten and walk up Odengatan.

Back home I take a shower and turn the TV on and flick through the channels but there's nothing interesting on and my whole body feels achy and I just don't have the energy to go to the tanning salon as I had planned. Check the time and it's half eight and I set the alarm clock to wake me up at 10.01 tomorrow then I go to bed.

When I get to Butler I see a waitress handing my parents the menu. They're sitting outdoors and I remove my shades and run my hand through my hair and walk up to them. My mother is wearing a blue blouse and a necklace I recognise and my father is wearing a white suit and blue tie.

'Well hello,' my mother says and smiles. I say hi and sit down.

'And how are you?' my dad asks and I say yeah ok, I'm fine and my mother says you look well.

I open the menu and glance at the meat courses and my mother asks my father if he's found anything and he nods slightly without looking at her and she smiles and says to the waitress that either way she would like a carafe of red in the meantime.

I say I want the steak from the specials board and a Ramlösa and my mother asks if I wouldn't like some wine and I say no thank you. My father looks at me and scratches his head and closes the menu and says well well.

The waitress brings the wine over and we order our food and my father hesitates for a bit about which beer to order but in the end he decides on a San Miguel but they've run out and he has an Old Gold instead and when the redhead waitress leans across the table to collect the menus I can see her large breasts. We're quiet for a moment and I watch a drunk across the street.

When my mum's first glass of red is finished the Ramlösa and the beer arrive and after my father has had a swig he leans back and finally breaks the silence:

'Have I told you I'm going to New York next week?' He looks at me.

'Really?' I say.

'Yes, well there's this business design congress.' He continues to tell me about some new project he's involved with but I'm not listening too carefully and I want my food to arrive.

We hardly say anything to each other whilst we're eating. My mother asks me twice if it's nice and the first time I say sure it's fine, and the second time, yes it's delicious.

When my father has finished eating he asks me as always if I perhaps have considered taking up studying and I say as always that yes, maybe and as always he tells me that he met some of his old student friends the other week and then he becomes nostalgic and talks about his jolly student life in the sixties.

Start work at half nine. I'm pretty much the only one of the staff who didn't go out the night before. Everyone's hungover and sluggish the first couple of hours and I find out that the police raided Pipeline last night and that Melody might be closing down.

Lunch starts and the daily special is fish burger and we joke about how disgusting it looks and hope it's not the staff food.

Half two I go home and sleep.

Wake up around seven and call Viktor and Micke.

We meet up at Konserthuscaféet at nine and Micke is particularly chirpy and silly. He talks fast and every other sentence is a seemingly relevant joke. Around eleven we head down to Dailys and there's already a queue but the bouncer knows Micke and waves us along.

We go to the bar and order three beers. Micke is still in a hysterical mood. It's like he's channelled only certain aspects of being high on speed. He tells a racist joke.

'A black guy goes into the job centre: Black guy: Hi, do you have a job for me? Job centre employee: Sure, you could become the CEO of Volvo if you want. Three hundred thousand a month, free car, free monthly trips to

America… Black guy: Seriously? You must be joking? Job centre employee: Yes, but you started it.'

We laugh uncontrollably and a barman that Micke knows laughs more than anyone. He walks across to the other side of the bar and I can see him retelling the story to some severe looking guy with extremely short hair in a white shirt and braces and a tie that he keeps touching. The guy laughs hysterically and slaps the counter a few times and has a swig of beer and when he's put it down he continues to laugh.

'I know another one that's even better,' says Micke and smiles and lights a cigarette.

'Do you know how many black people it takes to tarmac a road?'

'No,' Viktor says and I smile and shake my head.

'Depends on how thinly you slice them.'

Viktor giggles and I smile and Micke has a drag on his cigarette.

Two barstools become free and Viktor and I sit down and Micke says nice, sarcastically. We order another round of beers and Viktor asks Micke:

'That girl you pulled last night, who was that?'

'I don't know, she was working for some computer company, who cares, but…'

'And did you have a good time?' Viktor smiles.

'Well, no… but, well I was just going to tell you, but you know… it's a bit embarrassing…' He has another swig of beer. 'She pulls me and we go back to hers near Kungsholmstorg somewhere… and I have to be honest, she wasn't super hot. She was ok, no more, no less and I mean, a shag is always a shag even if I wasn't totally into it.

Anyway… I'm just about to unbutton my trousers and… well… she says you have a condom don't you?'

Viktor laughs and has another swig of beer and shakes his head and I light a new cigarette and laugh and try to imagine myself in the same situation.

'I was so fucking shocked you know,' he continues. So I simply say "Do you want me to keep my clothes on as well?"'

Both me and Viktor burst out laughing and I spill some beer and when Viktor's partially recovered he giggles:

'No really, what… no seriously, is that what you said?'

'So I do my trousers up again and stand up. I mean what the fuck, how can you be at the worst meat market in town, well almost, and pull some bloke and then start raving about condoms? I was so fucking pissed off, on top of not being particularly turned on. She said something about "but why are you so angry?" and I said nothing, I just put my shoes on and left. I mean, seriously…' He spreads his arms.

I'm listening to an old Soft Cell album and get nostalgic and look at old photos of my family and my school years. Wondering what everyone's doing now. I start sweating when I look at old photos of myself. I don't know why. I return all the old photos to the shoe box which says Adidas in white against a blue background and put it up on a shelf in the wardrobe. Start tidying up. Turn on the TV and turn the sound down. The program seems to be called "Weather In the Computer Age."

Feel really good about myself when I hoover the whole flat but it annoys me that I can't hear the music. Think for a while about finding my Walkman but can't be bothered. When I turn off the hoover I can hear Secret Life: "You think love is a dirty word, you pick up the phone and you ring when I'm at home and then you put it down and I'm reaching for my Valium. My secret life, living life on a knife-edge of life, tell my wife and she's just had a breakdown…"

I put the hoover away and lie down on the bed and watch TV. A man in a beard stands in front of a map of America and speaks but the music is louder than him and I try to read his lips. "Sleazy city, seedy films, breathing so heavy next to my neighbour." The telephone rings and I reach towards it but realise that I have to turn the music down and just as it rings for the third time I turn the volume down. I rush back and fall down on the bed and pick up.

'Heyyyy,' a girl says and giggles.

'Erm… hi,' I manage and I can't work out who it is and I'm watching TV. It looks like a space station but it's probably some computer centre for weather research.

'And how are you these days?' the voice says and I get nervous and my stomach hurts. I tend to feel like this when I don't know who I'm talking to. I reach for my cigarettes and can just about get them and I clear my throat and I say:

'Yeah, it's all good I guess.'

'Don't you want to know how I am?'

'Well, I suppose…' I can't see a lighter nearby. 'But who is this by the way?' I can hear my own nervous voice.

'I see, the great Don Juan has forgotten his old girlfriend?'

'Ah, ok, it's you… how are you?' I try to sound relieved. My forehead is getting sweaty and I'm hot and I undo my shirt and the pain in my stomach is almost unbearable but I can't start groaning so I lie down in a foetus position. It usually goes away then.

'I've just signed a contract with an agency in Paris,' she chirps and I think well you slut, whose cock did you suck to get that, but say:

'Wow, that's great.'

The pain subsides when I think of Lisa's body. She is actually good looking. Really hot.

'You sound weird?'

'I'm not feeling too well.

'Noo.' She says in a fake concerned way. 'So are you still at Hard Rock?'

'Yes, I'm afraid so,' I say and start wondering why she's calling me. We haven't spoken for at least six months. Ten months? Twelve?

'Why afraid so, is it that bad?'

'Yeah… or, I don't know… I think I should quit.'

'Really, and do what?'

'Don't know.'

It's quiet for nearly a minute and I feel stressed and I'm wondering if I dare leaving the phone to go and find a lighter. The program about weather computers ends and I can't stop thinking about her breasts and I imagine her giving me a blowjob.

'You don't want to meet up then?' she says all of a sudden and I'm thinking I wouldn't have had time to get a lighter.

'I don't know.'

'We could go out for dinner or something?'

'Mmm, that would…'

'What?'

'Oh, nothing.'

'I'm leaving for Paris soon.'

'Mmm.'

'How about just meeting up?'

'But, like, what would the point be?' I finally find the courage to say and I realise my cock is hard.

'Point? That's not what I meant?'

'What did you mean then?' I say and surprise myself that I sound so threatening.

'I was thinking…'

We fall silent and I'm wondering if she would notice if I had a wank. Why would I do that?

A film called "New Year's Nightmare" starts. I'm sweating and I'm thinking some coke now would be nice.

'Do you remember when…' I say without finishing the sentence.

'Are you still angry with me over that thing about Richard?'

'What, no, no I had totally forgotten about that. I don't even care.'

'But you were pretty upset about it right? I heard Marika say that she had seen you the same night and you…'

'What are you getting at?'

'I didn't think you would care… but like… I know it's been a year or so and… but can't we meet up and…'

'It was definitely a year ago and I think you're going to regret calling me today.' I sound really angry.

'I know, I should have called you ages ago but I think… why do you have to be so unpleasant? So you just don't want to see me?'

'I really don't know.'

'Shall I call again?'

'If you want to.'

'I want to.'

'Bye.' I hang up before she says bye.

I watch TV and a small child is in a bed and the door to the room opens and a massive shadow falls over the helpless baby.

I'm about to start crying and I have to take something. The tears pour out of me but I don't know why. Want to get Lisa out of my head. I had completely forgotten she

66

existed. I wasn't even in love. I don't care. Why am I crying now? She has to leave my head. Why is she calling now?

I get up and find a packet of Tavegyl on the shelf. Take three. Stomach pain returns. I don't understand this.

It's pissing down outside and the window I'm standing next to is open and I just can't stop myself from putting my hand out.

Feel some kind of relief when the rain hits my hand and I'm definitely coming down and I'm thinking that maybe I was a little bit too drunk tonight. I'm happy I didn't throw up anyway. One hand considerably chilled, I close the window.

Marie and Helene are giggling next to a pedestal outside the loos chopping out two new lines. I could easily have stared at Marie's body a little longer but a high and horny yuppie type starts dancing hysterically with his equally high and horny shag. "Unspeakable" by Killing Joke is blasting out of the speakers and the guitars pierce my ears. I'm wondering what year this song is from, 1980 or '81? The yuppie type sings along and seems nostalgic and blocks my view. The only thing I can see is Marie throwing her blonde hair back and laughing when this rock star whose name I can't recall pulls her close and leads her out of the room.

Realise that I'm the only one in the room not dancing. I slowly move away from the corner of this boring fuck fest where I hardly know anyone. A few people I recognise I guess, but the only ones I know the names of are Marie and Helene and I'm wondering how I ended up here. Only remember that we got in a cab from Caféet and I think we are in Surbrunnsgatan near the corner of Sveavägen. When I'm heading back into the next room I can't avoid hearing the rock star with long hair whose name I still can't recall:

'Well, you know, we're just finishing the final mix now.'

Neither can I avoid Marie's chirpy reply:

'Reaaallly, and what does it sound like?'

She looks extremely horny and the rock star has definitely pulled.

After a final confirmation that all the people here are boring I leave and stand in the doorway and know that it will take me roughly ten minutes to walk back in the pissing rain and that it will take roughly ten minutes for a cab to turn up. Decide to walk home in the pissing rain. Don't feel like talking to some annoying cab driver right now.

The clock at the Gustav Vasa church is showing four thirty-five when I reach Karlbergsvägen. One of those image-aware old age pensioners in rags is ahead of me collecting bottles and cans. They feel so incredibly sorry for themselves and they don't feel bad about flaunting it. They could be making money in an easier way but it seems like they want sympathy from the rest of the world.

I meet his saddened gaze when I pass him and I really force myself not to return a sympathetic look.

Back up in my flat I lie down in my bed full of popcorn and watch MTV. The new one from Simple Minds really is awful.

I wake up at three thirty and for a few minutes I'm convinced it's Wednesday when really it's Thursday. I drink half a litre of Bravo and remember I'm working this evening.

Smoke a cigarette and have a long much-needed shower.

By the time I've got dressed and dried my hair it's five o'clock. I stuff my shirt into a plastic bag and put my jacket on and by ten past five I'm on my way down to Hard Rock.

Finish my chiliburger with blue cheese and extra fries in ten minutes and flick through Expressen whilst I'm having my coffee.

I clock in at half five. A wonderful feeling of the calm that only exists in an almost empty restaurant prevails. Louise, who's been on my station before me, informs me that I only have one table and that they're already on their coffee. Unfortunately I know that within an hour all eight tables at my station will be full.

Micke asks if I want to have some coke after closing time. I tell him I feel a bit shit and that I can't make up my mind. Pour myself some coffee and sit down in the smoking room where two waitresses discuss last night's shags and whether the bouncer at Melody is good looking or sleazy.

When we've closed and counted the till and changed and I'm sitting on the counter eating the staff night food which is some kind of Jansson's temptation, Micke asks if I want some coke after all.

'Erm, don't know, I'm feeling a bit tired and it is a quarter to three after all.'

'So it's exactly what you need.'

'No but I'll join you if you're going to Pipeline.'

We've both got a beer in one hand and a cigarette in the other and laugh at the heavy metal guitarist who earlier the same day made a statement in the tabloids saying he's anti-drugs but here he is on stage at Pipeline playing air guitar, completely off his head. His girlfriend or shag is extremely embarrassed and puts her hands over her face while everybody else is laughing.

After another beer we call a cab and go out into the street. It's getting light.

The following afternoon I go over to Micke's and he's borrowed a video by some band called Psychic TV. We watch it and it's mostly noise and blood.

'You have to see this bit, it's the best,' he says and fast forwards to a song where some guy is in a bathtub filled with blood and he has electrodes stuck to his body. The picture is quite blurry and after a while a girl is stitching her own cunt together and I'm beginning to feel quite disgusted by the whole thing.

'It looks so fucking real,' Micke says and grins.

In the evening Mats and I go to a party at the Institute of Technology. It's absolutely rammed and very hot. Mats has had too much to drink and stumbles all over the place and is impossible to talk to. Last week we were here at another party and I met a girl called Sangita (… wonderful hooker name). She was incredibly beautiful and we decided to meet here again tonight.

The band goes on stage and runs through the usual covers. They start off with "Money For Nothing" and the only thing that keeps me watching is the back-up singers.

After a few numbers I go to the next floor down and wander around aimlessly and all of a sudden this Sangita turns up and with forced surprise I say heeey.

'Hi… hey look, I'm in a bit of a rush.' She smiles and walks on and I say ah ok quietly to myself and for a few seconds I feel like a complete idiot. But really, it doesn't matter and I head back upstairs and find Mats by a pillar trying to set off a fire extinguisher. I stop him just as he's pulled the pin out. He staggers and laughs.

I buy a beer and sit down at a table by the dance floor. Mats is trying to talk to a girl who looks mildly interested. When he tries to drag her to the dance floor she manages to break free and leaves. He comes over to me and spills half his beer when he sits down. A fat girl comes up to us and says she knows us. I don't think either of us has ever seen her but Mats says sure and starts chatting unintelligibly with her. I see Sangita in a corner with some guy I've never seen before.

Eventually we decide to leave and on the way down to the cloakroom Mats stumbles on the stairs and manages to grope two girls. It's incredibly embarrassing when he spits straight into the cloakroom and I'm glad we're not in a normal club. The cloakroom attendant doesn't notice and we get out and get into a cab.

Wake up at six. Watch a porn film and fast forward to all the blowjob scenes. Get up around seven and put on a Bowie record and eat crisp bread with gorgonzola. Watch a bad copy of "Un Chien Andalou" for what must be the fifth time. Around nine I call Micke. He says I'm an idiot for calling this early and hangs up. Wait five minutes and call him again. I pester him to meet up for a coffee.

Fifteen minutes later I've persuaded him and he says something about calling me and waking me up at seven some time.

Half ten I meet him at Strand Café in Norr Mälarstrand. Apparently they've just opened for the season and only half of the chairs are out.

Saturday nights before payday are always rubbish at work. Rubbish tips. All the hard-rockers are saving every last penny in order to get even more drunk. It's crowded. It's hot. It's simply hell.

Helene and I finish at midnight and I go with her to a party in Tegnérgatan.

Robert's there and he gives me some red wine and next to him there's a bloke who keeps spilling his vodka. When

I'm introduced to him I get vodka on my fingers and it stings.

I go to the loo to wash my hands and when I open the door I see Eva on the floor crying, surrounded by lots of jars and colourful pills. Nettan is squatting next to her and tries to talk to her.

'Eva's got a bit paranoid.' She turns to me and gives me a quick glance.

I hate situations like these and return to Robert and sit down next to him. My fingers are still stinging and "How Do You Think It Feels" by Lou Reed is on the stereo.

I think it's about one thirty when we arrive at Melody. Micke is there with some drunk girl I've never seen before. It's buzzing and I feel relaxed.

'There's no blue cheese on your fries,' Micke says.

I say nothing. I think about the dark brown wooden panels and the wooden benches. Apparently it's some special kind of wood, all Hard Rocks in the world have to use the same type of wood. Some story has it that they first used a different kind of wood when they opened in Stockholm and when the inspectors came from America they went mental and ripped it all out.

'Fuck, no blue cheese,' Micke says with a confused expression on his face.

I say nothing. Think about all the sweat and all the dirty clothes that have chafed against this wooden bench I'm sitting on.

I can't even touch the burger or the fries so I light a cigarette. Feel sick when I look at all the blue cheese dressing he's spilt on the table. I blow smoke at the framed Pink Floyd gold album.

'Light beer?'

'Yes,' I say and realise I'm really thirsty. Micke jumps out of the chair and almost dances across to the light beer tap in the bar.

On the way back, a beer in each hand, he hugs Fia who's coming out with some food. She smiles.

When we leave it's getting dark outside. It's about ten I guess. We decide to go for a bottle of wine at Britannia.

It's fairly quiet and we sit down on the bar stools next to the jukebox. Micke hits the wine the hardest as always and says suddenly Midsummer is only a month away and I ask him what he's doing and he says there's always a party somewhere. My fingers are unusually white and I drum along to "Rock the Night" on the table. Watch a guy with long hair at another table idly singing along. His lips are moving "Rock now, rock the night early in the morning light". The bottle is empty after only twenty minutes even though I've only had one glass. Micke asks if we should order another or head over to Collage straight away. My white fingers continue to drum.

'It's only half ten I guess,' he continues.

I make a strained face.

'What's up with you? What about Patricia? They do a happy hour on Sunday evenings. Or Caféet?'

'I think I'll head home,' I say thinking that my fingers are drumming in blue cheese dressing; splosh... splosh... splosh... splosh...

'What the fuck, I'm calling Tobbe and Viktor.' He's gone a few minutes and comes back laughing.

'You should have heard Viktor, totally plastered, completely off his head... he's off to Collage in an hour.'

He laughs and I smile. Totally wasted, he grins but then he straightens up a bit and asks if I want to share another bottle. I say I only got tipped two hundred and he says I'm buying and I say ok.

We start on the second bottle and I ask if he got hold of Tobbe.

'No, I don't know where he is, I haven't got hold of him in days. He hasn't been at work either has he?'

'I don't know.'

'No.'

'I don't think so.'

At quarter past eleven the second bottle is finished and as usual I've only had one glass. Micke is getting a bit stressed but I bum a cigarette off him and persuade him to wait until I've finished smoking.

Half eleven we split up by Odenplan. I'm getting hungry and get a take away pizza. On my way back I run into a loud gang of Turkish hip hop guys. Reminds me of something a waitress, Carina, said earlier in the day: Almost all Turkish guys are rapists, it's kind of part of their culture. Very animatedly she told me how many times she'd been chased. Even if they don't want to rape me they look really threatening. I'm wondering how it would feel if one of them kicked my Cacciatora up into my face. The melted cheese slowly running down my face.

Next day at work I check this week's rota and realise that Tobbe is not down for any shifts at all.

I work a long lunch and as usual you work your butt off between eleven and one thirty and then sit down and have coffee until six when you clock out and eat. Staff food is "Chinese stew" and I have two massive servings.

When I get home I try to call Tobbe but no one picks up. Get in the car and drive over to Viktor. It takes ages for him to open the door, every time I bang on the door he says wait two seconds. When he finally opens the door he's soaking wet and tells me excitedly about a new computer game he's copied from some guy. Whilst he's talking he goes into the kitchen to get two beers and hands me one.

'You have to watch,' he says and sits down in front of the screen. 'You're this guy, Larry Laffer.' A bloke with a small body and large head appears on the screen. 'You're supposed to go to this bar and order a whiskey that you give to a drunk who's passed out in the loos.'

'Mmm,' I nod.

'The drunk gives you a remote control and you enter the room next to the bar and there's this black, fat pimp. You turn on the TV,' he points at the screen. 'When you finally find the right channel... you write "use remote..." the channel showing a porn film, the pimp sits down in front of the TV and you bolt up the stairs and there's a hooker on the bed... hang on, why don't you take over...' He gets up and I sit down in front of the computer.

'Let's see what you'll do now then...' he giggles.

I write "Fuck girl" on the computer and it replies "Don't be so rude" and I write "Undress girl" and I watch this hooker getting undressed. I write "Undress" and Larry Laffer takes his clothes off and then I write "Fuck girl". A black vibrating box censors the bed and Viktor and I giggle.

'You'll die soon,' Viktor grins wickedly. 'I made the same mistake in the beginning. You have to buy condoms in the bar before you fuck her otherwise you die as she's got Aids or something.'

'What? That sucks.'

'Mmm,' he giggles.

I get up and Viktor sits down and starts the game again.

'You haven't heard from Tobbe recently, have you?' I ask.

'No, but give him a ring.'

I call but no one picks up and I wonder why he's not even got his answering machine on. Viktor is back with the pimp and writes "Fuck you, you blackpimp!" but the computer asks "What's a blackpimp?"

I somehow feel uneasy when we arrive at the party where Micke is picking up some speed. It's about five when we ring the doorbell and a guy with a straggly black fringe that obscures his eyes opens the door. "Venus In Furs" by Velvet Underground is playing loudly and Micke chirps hiya and tries to shake the hand of this guy who's maybe around twenty-two twenty-three and who makes no effort to extend his hand. I can see his lips moving as if saying hi but it's impossible to hear over the music "Kiss the boots of shiny shiny leather… shiny leather in the dark." Micke leans forward and says something to the guy and when he replies I fix my eyes on a large silver cross around his neck. I'm thinking this is not your normal goth party, or is it? The guy shuffles away in his flapping long black shirt and torn black trousers. Micke gives me a sign to follow and we enter a fairly big smoky room and at first I can't see anything, only a few glimmers of light through the blinds. After a while I can make out some guys on a sofa. One of them seems to be asleep and the other three are smoking and staring blankly into nothing. A feeling of fear comes over me and I wish this guy would arrive and give Micke his speed so we can get out of here. Somebody's apparently pressed repeat on the CD player and as soon as Venus In

Furs finishes it starts again. Micke points at a poster on the wall but I can't work out what it is. Below the poster a guy on the floor is leaning against the wall with a bottle of wine next to him and his eyes are closed or he's sleeping. When Venus In Furs starts for the third time I ask Micke what's taking them so long but before he can answer the guy with the fringe arrives back and gives him a packet of Marlboro and Micke smiles and slaps him lightly on the shoulder and it actually looks like he's smiling when he nods.

When we're finally out again we're blinded by the daylight and Micke says nice guys eh?

'It kind of puts you off downers seeing those guys,' I say and smile. 'And I wouldn't exactly buy speed off one of them.'

'True… but they're not as weird as they seem. Lasse is completely normal the rest of the time, it's only when they get into that shit they come across as a bit annoying.'

'It seemed like they were total junkies to me.'

Micke laughs.

'They've just been given some opium from a guy who's returned from China, that's all. And so they smoke opium for days and listen to weird music and read stuff by someone called Alistair Crowley, lots of eccentric magic stuff and devil worship and that kind of thing, I mean, you'd be pretty gone yourself after a while.'

'Don't feel like trying.'

'Lasse is so fucking well set up, his old man owns some huge company and he sends cheques every month, he got given that flat and a Ferrari and all that, it was Lasse I borrowed that Psychic TV video from by the way.'

'Mmm, if you watch that stuff all day long…

On the tube on the way home a guy with a limp approaches every single person in the carriage asking them if they've got any small coins for the train to Södertälje and when he reaches Micke he replies, sorry mate, I've only got lots of big ones. Not particularly funny.

Micke gets to mine around six and we drink two Green Pearl and get a cab to Djursholm where Linda's having a birthday party in her parents' villa.

No one answers when we ring the doorbell. Loud music is coming from the back and we go around the house. A temporary bar is erected by the pool and "Rosanna" by Toto blasts out from two giant speakers.

'Yeah, she's clearly going out with a bouncer,' Micke says and laughs. Out of maybe thirty people around the pool at least ten are as big as houses.

We go up to the bar and say hello to Linda's brother who's acting barman. We get a glass of champagne each and sit down by the pool. I stare at the bouncer gang who all look like huge babies and are play-fighting with each other all the time. I try to work out which one Linda's going out with but they all look the same.

Nettan comes up to us and says hi and she drinks San Miguel and smokes and when I ask what happened to Eva last Saturday she says, yeah, we sorted it out, she'll probably pop by later.

"Electrified" by Electric Boys is playing and Nettan looks excited when she says:

'Conny might be coming tonight.'

'Conny?' Micke and I ask in unison.

'Yeah, Conny Blomqvist,' she sighs.

'Oh right, him,' Micke smiles ironically.

'Oh stop it, the singer from Electric Boys for fuck's sake.'

'Mmm,' I say and Micke nods.

'Have you seen Linda by the way?' We shake our heads. 'She was just sorting something out but she'll be back soon… don't know that many people here really…'

'Uh-uh,' I say and slowly shake my head.

I see Viktor and Robert and Tom arriving in the garden and go straight up to the bar and Micke and I go over there too.

'I didn't think you were allowed to work in a bar when you're under eighteen,' Viktor says and smiles at Linda's brother who's fifteen (or sixteen).

Tom says hello and asks:

'How come there's so many bodybuilders here?'

'Linda's dating a bouncer, did you not know?'

'Oh shit… well they seem like a nice and relaxed bunch of guys…' he says and smiles. 'But… how do you feel about that, weren't you two steady fuck friends?'

'Mmm… well, I don't really care,' I say and wonder if I really don't… No, I don't. Linda comes out and we all hug her and say happy birthday and everything and Micke asks: So how does it feel to be twenty-one? Just to have something to say.

Her bouncer comes up and he's wearing aviator sunglasses and she introduces him to us. He's called Anders and we smile awkwardly when we shake hands. I wonder if he knows I've fucked his girlfriend more times than he has?

'Why weren't you at Dailys last night? There was a fashion show and Anna was in it. You should have seen it, she had amazing clothes on and it was rammed,' Linda says. Top night.

Anna worked in Hard Rock six months ago and we used to bring her to parties and she and Linda became friends. I believe that out of the five of us, Viktor is the only one who hasn't slept with her. At one point there were rumours that the head manager fucked her in the office.

'I was working,' Micke says and has a sip of white wine and I open a beer and pretend I didn't hear the question.

Anders, the bouncer, takes Linda's hand and steers her away and they sit down on some garden chairs. The rest of us look at each other and Tom says what the fuck's wrong with her?

Micke is drinking champagne uncontrollably and around half ten he's getting pretty pissed and it's starting to get dark and Tom is trying to persuade Robert to walk up to one of the body builders and ask him if he's got any steroids to sell.

Suddenly everyone's yelling, drowning out "Calling Out to Carol" and some of the bouncers throw one of their friends in the pool. When he gets out he pretends he's pissed off but I wouldn't be surprised if he's secretly pretty pleased since he can walk around flexing his muscles in nothing but boxers now.

Nettan's talking about this Conny Blomqvist and smokes joint after joint and is giggly and annoying and seems worried that he's not coming. Micke and I are sitting by the side of the pool and talk about which waitresses have slept with which heavy metal singers and he suggests that it must be a job requirement:

'If you give a few hard-rockers a blowjob this weekend you can start waitressing on Monday,' he says and we giggle idly.

Around half eleven everybody starts talking about where to go and I just want to go home and sleep.

Eventually we end up in Cosmo Club in Sigtunagatan and it's the same as all of these shitty acid house clubs; same people, same music, half full and half boring. The only good thing about it is that the bouncer mafia have all gone to the opening of DIO 29 instead. Me, Robert, Micke, Tom, Viktor, Nettan and Linda and two of her friends from the party who I think are models but whose names I can't recall move two tables together where we sit down with a beer each and no one seems particularly up for it apart from Robert who's pretty high. Don't know what on but can't be bothered asking.

I go to the loo and an acid house tune comes through the vents and the metallic bassline is creating an awful racket when I go into one of the booths. The floor is wet and I remember that one of my soles has a hole in it. I piss away sick from the toilet seat and stand in a strange position to avoid getting my right foot wet. Go back to our table where only Nettan and Linda and a couple of dopey goths are left. I ask where the others are and Linda laughs and says they're pretty plastered, embarrassingly they were off dancing, all of them.

I do a round and then sit down and notice that Nettan seems interested in these goths. When the others return

88

from the dancefloor there's talk about going to Pipeline and I decide to go home.

We get out into the street and they fairly quickly get a cab and I start walking slowly up Odengatan and I don't know why but I start thinking about the first time I slept with Linda.

I remember it was one of those nights you imagine all nights are like in the daytime. Romantic and wet asphalt and neon like electric eels outside the cab window. Remember we were in Patricia. It was maybe a year ago. I had been doing some shifts at Hard Rock last term at high school and Linda had been studying physics for a year and this evening was the first time we'd seen each other in months. Remember I was sat at a table by myself and was too drunk, when I closed my eyes everything started spinning and I was constantly trying to focus on something to avoid the nausea. I was looking down on the dance floor and I remember a waitress I had been working with at Casa Bianca, who had now started at Patricia, came up to me and told me it was last orders and did I want anything else.

Realise I've been talking to myself out loud and I have an urge to talk about it as if Linda were walking beside me.

…and you know, I was so disgusted by being so drunk, like, I sat there inhaling deeply, smoke and perfume and booze and everything just felt so shit and I got up and went to the cloakroom and just as I gave the cloakroom attendant the fiver I heard your voice behind me and you said "you were supposed to let me know" and I said "sorry" and you said "I'm coming home with you" and I said "cab, right?" and it was like in some bad movie. In the cab you got a piece of paper out and wrote the new code for your buzzer and your address on it

with an eye liner that must have cost hundreds and you gave me the note without saying anything. We went past McDonalds where gangs of blonde sixteen-year olds were hanging out and you giggled and said "that's right up your street isn't it?" and I just nodded. Apart from that we were silent almost the whole ride and of course the cab driver had country music on and I think you had a hand on my thigh almost all the way. On the stairs I was getting horny and I remember you got the keys from me and opened the door (was I really that drunk?). You smiled your most seductive smile and I was so grateful that you didn't want to drink tea and light candles and all that. I think we only had a glass of water and you were wearing knickers and some kind of vest and I tried to get into your eyes with my tongue but you just giggled and I pulled up your upper lip with my little finger and was only thinking flesh on flesh and saliva on saliva. You unbuttoned and started sucking and I had two fingers inside you and you smelled of body lotion and Chanel. Do you remember we ended up doing it on the floor in the hallway?

It's half two and the lunch rush is over and Micke and I are talking to Jonas who's the manager today. He's very lively and jolly and all of a sudden he says follow me and we follow him past the kitchen porter where the Turkish guy (Ibrahim?) is standing by the rumbling dishwasher and we continue to the staff loos. The three of us enter and Jonas locks the door:

'Not a word to anyone about this.'

He pulls out a joint from a cigarette case and lights it and has three deep puffs on it and passes it to me. It does the rounds a few times and we all giggle.

When we get back into the restaurant Kicki comes up to me.

'Where the fuck have you been, we've got guests at 32.'

'Mmm,' I giggle.

It's an American couple who both want the chiliburger and bottle of red and I say yeah, sure and I feel pretty high. They look at me slightly confused and I grin and try not to burst out laughing.

When I serve the fat couple pudding, two giant ice creams, I can't stop giggling hysterically and the grey haired man in aviator sunglasses asks for the bill.

389 kronor. I get given a five hundred note and when I start handing him the change he says it's fine. I laugh and say thank you very much thank you and go downstairs to tell Micke I got a one hundred and eleven kronor tip and we start discussing whether they miscounted or if it was because I was nice.

'Well you know. Americans like drugs,' Micke says and we laugh.

I'm in bed watching two films on the cable channel. The first is about a family moving into a haunted house. One family member after another dies and gravestones appear in the living room. The other is a Vietnam war film about some American soldiers getting lost in the jungle who burn every village they get to and in the end they're rescued.

Around four, when I'm just on my way down to Metro to get a few things, the phone rings and it's Lisa.

'How are you?' she asks and I instinctively feel I shouldn't be talking to her.

'Well... I'm in a hurry... meeting a friend in town.'

'Yeah right.' She knows I'm lying.

'Why don't you call another day?'

Out in the street I feel nauseous and I tell myself it's because of the bright light and that it will stop if I go for a little walk. On a meter box someone has fly posted two of the same posters next to each other saying "Jesus is coming. Are you ready?" I stop and look at the posters a moment. "Jesus is coming. Are you ready?" Go to Metro and do the shopping.

It's a rainy Saturday when I wake up around eleven and for some reason it feels like it's a totally pointless day. Go into the kitchen and remember I actually bought coffee when I went shopping so I turn the coffee machine on and get a large bowl of ice cream and make two sandwiches.

Whilst I'm waiting for the coffee to get ready I stand by the window and look at the trees in the yard. That uneasy feeling mixed with fear comes over me when I watch the branches. It's pissing down and I can't stop thinking about dead and bloody people hanging upside down completely drenched. There's three of them and water mixed with blood is dripping from their dangling arms.

Lie down in bed and watch a few music videos whilst having breakfast. When I've finished eating the melted ice cream I switch to Filmnet where a film called "Revenge" is just starting. It's pretty rubbish but I finish watching it and then I pull the covers over me and try to sleep but I can't.

Switch over to MTV and watch a Paul McCartney video and then one by The Cure and then an old one by Eurythmics and then one by Bon Jovi and then one by Elvis Costello and then one by Fine Young Cannibals.

I try to sleep again but I can't. I'm thinking of that video by The Cure where the singer is lying on a bed under a thick spider web and then I wonder how long I would have to lie here until I was covered in a thick spider web and dust.

I almost call Micke to see if he's got any Valium or Barbitur or Stesolid or Mogadon to sell me but remember he's working and it feels wrong taking them anyway. Downers are just so destructive.

Watch three films back to back and none of them is particularly good and I'm wondering if there's something wrong with me. I used to think most films were ok.

The last one is some kind of action war movie and when the Americans have blown up the Japanese military base in the final scene I go into the kitchen and stand by the window and light a cigarette but move away immediately so I don't have to look at the dangling arms.

Have a glass of water and go back to bed and watch a few music videos and then a film and when it's finished I feel it might be possible to fall asleep.

It's one of those Sunday afternoons that feels like it happens in slow motion and Micke and I take the tube to Östermalmstorg and go over to Tom's in Linnégatan. He opens the door dressed in Bermuda shorts and he looks like he's spent most of last week in the tanning salon. Micke and Tom sit down on the living room sofa and I sit down in an armchair opposite and look at the aquarium on a steel and wooden structure in front of the window. Tom's smoking and looking through his phone book and Micke is playing with the remote control and turns the TV behind me on and off repeatedly. Nobody's saying anything and I look at the aquarium and then the TV and Micke is fiddling about with the buttons and the news reader goes from being black and white to green in the face. He turns the volume up and there's a hoarse voice over the noise and I look at the aquarium again. Six, maybe six seven centimetres long, shiny orange fat fish swim around and around. They all have a sad and empty gaze and they constantly look through the glass and I wonder if they realise how bored they really are. I suppose it hadn't been much fun out in the sea either. Every day they get fish food and then they just swim around and around and look through the glass.

The noise from the TV is back on after being quiet for a minute or so and I look at Micke and then at the screen.

'Oh for fuck's sake stop doing that,' Tom says and a warm feeling that someone is finally saying something comes over me. Micke turns the volume down but continues to distort the picture. It's silent for a minute or so. Eventually Tom says:

'Fucking hell, can't you just stop?'

Micke turns the TV off and grins and runs a hand through his hair and puts the remote down with the other.

'What about doing something tonight?' I ask.

'I've heard Patricia is going to be busy,' Micke says and runs his hand through his blonde hair again.

'Mmm,' Tom lights a cigarette and throws his phone book down on the table next to the remote control.

'I feel like some speed,' Micke smiles.

'Do you have some?' Tom asks.

'Sure.'

'For us too?'

'Ha… the kingpin himself asks me…'

'Oh shut up will you, I don't have any at home… nothing, and you…'

'Hey, I was only joking.'

It's quiet for a few seconds.

'So do you have some for us?'

'Yeah, it's cool.'

'So, what are we doing? Have you eaten?' He looks at me then Micke.

'Who needs food?' Micke smiles and holds his bag of speed up.

'Why don't we go to Östergök for some dinner, have some beers and then come back here?' Tom suggests. 'Unless the speedfreak here is suffering from withdrawal…' He looks at me and glances mockingly at Micke.

'Stop it.'

'Ok, let's go. I'll just get changed.'

Whilst he's in the bedroom I watch the fish in the aquarium again and Micke lights a cigarette and flicks through the TV-express.

At Östergök we all have Greek salad and three beers each and when we get back up to Tom's flat it's about half nine.

Micke sits down in the same place on the sofa and gets the speed out and I roll up a tenner and Tom squats down between the aquarium and the end of the table and watches.

'I don't want too much,' I say and Micke says you're not having much anyway and chops out a line that would keep me up for two days.

'About half of that is enough.' I snort a third of the line in two goes and hand the tenner over to Tom. He closes his eyes and snorts roughly as much as me and looks up and makes a face and wrinkles his nose and passes the note to Micke. He puts some more out and snorts it all in one go.

After about twenty minutes Micke has that strange look in his eyes and he starts talking about some video he's seen and I listen attentively even though I don't really care and I can feel I'm getting high.

In the cab to Patricia Micke is in the front seat and tells the cab driver that he used to drive a cab but he stopped after he ran over a mother and her two children ("you know, there was blood everywhere") and Tom and I are in the back giggling and talking nonsense.

The cab driver who's in his forties doesn't seem to find it funny and Micke grins and changes the subject and asks him if he sometimes fucks his female customers ("...a quickie in the back seat is never wrong...") but he doesn't reply and Micke bursts out laughing.

At Patricia we meet Robert and Linda and her bouncer and Helene and Louise and Nettan and Marie and Anna and Fredrik and me and Fredrik and Robert who's wearing a new Armani suit go upstairs to the deck and after a while we go over to the railing. Some girls in black leggings are next to us and point down to the quayside and talk animatedly. We look down and there's a drunk or a junkie on the quay squirming in his own sick and I can't know for sure but it doesn't look like he's conscious even though he continues to throw up and shake his head. I wonder why we didn't see him when we arrived in the cab. A few more people arrive and one of the girls in the black leggings repeats "god it's sooo disgusting" and has a sip of her spritzer and I stare at her butt and realise I have a hard on.

We go downstairs again and watch the dance floor and Micke is dancing hysterically with some girl from a model agency and some house song I recognise but I can't remember the name of is playing.

Even when I'm high I usually have a pretty good idea what time it is but suddenly the music stops and the whole place lights up and the sound of everyone heading to the cloakroom is ringing in my ears and I want to stop being high. Fredrik comes up to me and asks if I'm working tomorrow and I say nope and he says but I'll see you around and I nod and say sure.

It's three thirty when we drive along the quayside and far across the water is Gröna Lund and I remember that I forgot to check if that junkie was still there.

When I get home I think I've come down. I undress and lie down in bed and my body feels pretty tired but I'm wide awake. I start talking incoherently to myself and turn the TV on and one of the cable channels is showing a love story that's probably incredibly boring but I talk to the different characters and watch it until the end and then get up and turn the stereo on and start washing up and wipe the kitchen table. I could do with some Valium but I don't have any so I have some Tavegyl and then I go to the loo and rinse my face in cold water a few times. Get a cloth from the kitchen and start cleaning the bathroom shelves and when I've done that I go back to bed. The alarm clock is saying 07.38 and even though I know I'll only sleep a few hours all I want is to sink into a deep sleep. Watch some music videos. Have no idea how many, twenty-five thirty maybe. Smoke some cigarettes and think that I might be able to relax a little.

Feel really good about myself for getting up at nine thirty. Drink some juice and read the first part of DN and the post brings a cheque from my dad for two thousand. It usually happens when he's done some good business deal. I guess he feels guilty for making so much money.

I get ready and take the car to town and park in Nybrogatan. Head over to Sturegallerian and the record shop and start rummaging through the new stuff but I can't find anything I want. It's half eleven and I'm hungry. Have the salad special at Café Gateau and read the first page of a Svenska Dagbladet someone's left behind.

When I get home Linda has left a message on the answering machine and I call her back but no one picks up. Lie down on the bed and stare at the ceiling. Smoke some cigarettes and watch the smoke slowly swirling towards the ceiling. Try to blow smoke rings but fail as usual. Stand up and feel dizzy and a severe headache comes over me. I feel pretty shit. Put on Jesus and the Mary Chain and hum along to the words: "I'm going to the darklands, to talk in rhyme with my chaotic soul. As sure as life means nothing and all things end in nothing And heaven I think is too close to hell I want to go I want to move."

Consider going shopping but change my mind and turn the stereo off and the TV on. When I've watched a few music videos the phone rings and I pick up after two signals and it's Lisa.

'How's it going?' she asks and I see her face in front me.

'Ok I guess, how about you?'

'Good… what are you up to tonight?'

'Nothing special.'

'Do you want to grab a beer?'

'Mmm, maybe,' I say.

'Are you listening to the radio?'

'No, why?'

'I was just wondering if you heard the one that's on now… if you knew what it was called, this one by Dusty Springfield… you know, the new one.'

'Do you mean…'

'Is it called Mirrors?'

'I don't know. It's that soundtrack to that new film… what's it called… "Scandal" isn't it?'

'Maybe… she sings it with the Pet Shop Boys.'

'Mmm.'

'Maybe… oh never mind… so do you want to meet up then?'

'Mmm, sure.'

'Tranan at eight?'

'Sure.'

'Ok… bye.'

'Bye.'

When I get to Tranan, Lisa's already sitting down at a table at the far end and when I see her my stomach hurts and

I don't really know why. I go up to her and say hi and put my cigarettes on the table and go over to the bar. The barman is playing "Competition Is None" by Rob n Raz and I order a Guinness. Lisa's having white wine and she's brought her portfolio. She starts telling me about Paris and about the agency she's signed up to and about the photographer, Luigi, who's given her "sooo much support". She starts going through her portfolio and shows me some new photographs of herself (that Luigi has shot) and tells me what magazines she's been in recently. I wonder if she's brought the portfolio just to show me or if there's really some other reason she just happened to have it with her. She is insanely beautiful and I wonder how many times she's slept with this Luigi character and she talks about some modelling Svengali who drugged all his models and then raped them all and about a film team who filmed it all and sent the tape to Eileen Ford who stopped all contact with the Svengali which in turn led to a pair of Swedish agencies getting into trouble etc. There's a lot of intrigue and it's just boring and I watch her fingers and nod whilst she rabbits on.

Eventually we decide to go to hers and I guess we both knew that would be the case. The only thing she says in the cab is that she's leaving the day after tomorrow.

When I fuck her she groans as loud and in the same way as I remember and she mumbles "fuck me, harder, oh my god" etc and it's like a porn film. She scratches my back and it feels like she's writing her initials on my back. She comes twice and I wonder how many times Luigi makes her come and then I come inside her and she smiles with

her eyes half closed and I lie down on my back next to her.
Look at the window and the blinds.

*I remember I used to lie here in the morning and it used to feel like
the wind blew straight through me even when I was under the covers.
Remember how the faint light used to filter through the blinds onto
her body.*

*I remember one morning especially when I pretended I was asleep
and discreetly squinted at her and how she got up and looked at me for
a long time and then put her dressing gown on. I remember how she sat
down at the desk and wrote something on a piece of paper and I still
pretended to be asleep. Remember how she held the paper up in front
of her and then crumpled it up and turned around on the chair and
spread her legs and pressed her breasts against the back. Remember
how she went to the loo after a while and flushed. Remember
wondering if she flushed down the piece of paper. Remember how for
weeks I wondered what she wrote. Remember how the red digits on the
alarm clock said 07.13 that morning. Remember thinking it would
go off at 07.16 and that it had been doing that for weeks. Remember
how she went to the bathroom 07.15 and I was thinking that she did
that so she wouldn't have to hear the alarm going off. Remember how
she got out of the shower and played Dabello or Michael Jackson or
Bryan Ferry or something. Remember how I was lying on my back
smoking when she stood in front of me and took her dressing gown
off. Remember how she sat down in bed and ran her hand through my
hair. Remember how I smiled at her. Remember how she smiled at me.*

I'm thinking about that morning. It must have been
special. The last morning? "Last Morning", reminds me
of that awful song by Niklas Strömstedt.

Wake up in an empty bed and the bathroom stinks of body lotion and I go to the kitchen and feel relieved she's not at home. Find a note on the kitchen table where it says she's at a photo shoot and to call her. She's written down the number for MIKAS who she works for and the agency in Paris (illegible, V.I.P. models?) and her own. I write a message (not going to call) and I think about how beautiful she is and how the sun is shining through the window and that I feel pretty good after all. Get dressed and stand in the doorway looking at the empty bed. Trying to sort my hair out then leave. Östermalmstorg is beautiful and it's two o'clock.

Get down to Hard Rock at seven on the dot. Get changed and take over station four where a new waitress called Karin has been during the day. There's a young couple at table twenty-six and I take their order and put it through the machine. Then walk over to the kitchen and ask for staff food. One of the chefs, whose name I can never remember, puts a plate of rice and some meat stew in the microwave. I eat standing outside the kitchen when Pierre, the restaurant boss, walks past. He's in his thirties, blond and thinning and hated by everyone because he sees himself as some hospitality business genius.

'First of all, we don't eat out here,' he says authoritatively and looks at me spitefully. 'Second, you should have eaten before you started your shift.'

'But I only have one table and…'

'That makes no difference… There's always something that needs doing, filling up ketchup bottles for example,' he continues bluntly and holds up a ketchup bottle in front of me. 'Does this look right to you?'

I go into the coffee room to finish my dinner. Someone (Micke?) has torn a picture of deformed animals from Chernobyl out of a newspaper and underneath someone has written something illegible. Helene is talking to Malin and pulls hard on her Blue Blend.

'…and when she sat down with you know, he couldn't face… well, anyway, I mean he thinks he can sleep with me when it suits him, I mean, he's not thaaat fucking famous…' Helene goes on and Malin nods occasionally and I eat my dinner and try to stop thinking about the deformed animals and wonder if they're talking about the singer from Electric Boys.

When I've finished eating and head back to the kitchen with my plate "Get Nasty" by Electric Boys comes on of course, "I ain't got nine lives even though I'm a real cool cat".

It's one of those really hot days in May and I find an old Psychedelic Furs album that I listen to all morning. Feel guilty about not being out in this beautiful weather. Lie on the bed and watch the TV with no sound on and listen to the record over and over again. Linda calls and asks if I want to have a drink at Yo-Yo. Their outdoor seating area has just opened. There are old WWII movies in slow motion on the TV and I'm struggling to concentrate on what she's saying.

At Yo-Yo Linda has a beer and I have a diet Coke and she asks if I've seen Tobbe recently and I say not for ages.

When I get back home I put the Psychedelic Furs album on again and somehow it feels like this day never happened. A kind of transition in vacuum, from yesterday until tomorrow… or no, that's ridiculous. Remember Lisa is off to Paris today. I think it feels good.

Get woken up at ten by a phone call from my mum.

'Hi, it's only your old mother.'

'Yeah… hi.'

'You weren't sleeping were you?'

'No.'

'Did you get the cheque today?'

'Mmm… I don't know… I don't think the post has arrived.'

'Have you not looked?... You must have heard if the post arrived.'

'Yeah.'

'And has it?'

'I don't know.'

'Oh yes, I was going to tell you, I'm off to New York this afternoon.'

'Really?'

'Yes… isn't it amazing?'

'Yes.'

'Dad's already there but you knew that right?'

'Yes.'

'I'll visit him and then we fly down to Barbados for a week.'

'Right. Fun.'

'So I thought you might want some holiday money too if you're doing something.'

'Mmm, maybe I will, thank you.'

'I'm in a bit of a hurry… but I'll call you when I get there.'

'Ok, do that.'

'Have a lovely time.'

'And you.'

'Alright then… Bye.'

'Bye.'

'Bye.'

'Bye.'

I get up and have a shower and go to the hallway and true enough there is an envelope with a cheque in it.

I don't really feel like going anywhere but I'm curious to know what kind of holiday you could buy for three thousand anyway.

Get dressed and go down to Metro and do the shopping and when I get up I make myself a proper breakfast and read DN thoroughly and when I'm done it's one o'clock.

Go down to the off licence in Odengatan by the junction of Sigtunagatan. Get in a queue with four people in front of me.

I don't know if it's true but someone said that this branch of Systembolaget is the only one in town that hasn't introduced ticket machines and signs with red dots displaying the number being served. The guy in front of me has damaged pale blue hair that looks like it might have been a mohican a long time ago. He's wearing a t-shirt with the sleeves cut off. On the back there's a lot of pictures and bits of text printed. NOW! THE EXCITEMENT REALLY BEGINS! It says at the top. A jolly looking spaceman is standing next to it and behind him are silhouettes of machine guns with bayonets. Below the text are two small pictures next to each other. One depicts some bombed out houses and the other a guy walking along a beach. Below the pictures in big letters: MEET THE MASTERS OF WORLD WAR III and: WHITEWASH HISTORY and below that a fairly big picture of missiles with Adolf Hitler and Reagan inserted at the bottom of the missiles. Hitler smiles and Reagan (I think it's Reagan) seems to be smiling but it's hard to be sure. The t-shirt looks like it's been washed many times but across the whole back is printed in big red letters: DEAD KENNEDYS. I know I've heard them somewhere but can't think of a particular song.

The guy with the pale blue hair and the Dead Kennedys t-shirt buys four Kronenburg and two bottles of Donelli Lambrusco. He pays and the checkout girl looks at me and I say four Henric Åkesson and she asks me for ID and I show her my driving licence and she says thanks and goes to get my order. I'm wondering why the uniforms at Systembolaget are so ugly. The yellowy brown shirts and trousers and the green velvet slipover.

She comes back and I pay 260 kronor and I have to put the bottles of sparkling wine in two plastic bags myself.

When I get home I put the bottles in the fridge and put on a cassette with Billy Idol but when the song begins I realise how bored of it I am and turn it off.

Thinking about calling someone but both Fredrik and Micke are working. I call Tobbe but as usual no one picks up. I call Linda and her machine says "well hellooo… is that you… I'm not at home but say something sweet after the beep" and after the beep I say hi it's Johan but I didn't want anything in particular. Call Mats but no answer. Call Tom and his machine says angrily "what do you want?" and after the beep I say nothing and hang up.

Contemplate renting some videos but realise I have to go to the bank in that case to cash the cheque I got and can't be bothered.

Go to the window and light a cigarette. Look at the trees and the branches that look like humans.

Look at the trees in the backyard and the branches that look like human arms. Someone should chop those trees down. I'm wondering if any of my neighbours feel as uneasy about these trees as I do. I guess most people in the block are too old to see or feel anything.

Feel idle and walk back and forth in the flat a few times and then into the bathroom where I stand in front of the mirror and stare at myself. Think about calling Tobbe but he's probably not in.

Lisa pops into my head.

The room was starkly lit. At least that's how I remember. All the lights were on and it was completely silent. I squinted in the light from the bedside lamp which I had placed in front of my face. I was half lying down on the bed with my legs stretched out and my back against the wall. She was on the floor in front of me. Her knickers were pulled down to her knees. Her lilac t-shirt advertising LdB body care came down to her thighs and obscured the hand she was masturbating with. I had a hard on and started moving my foreskin slowly up and down. She had a firm grip of my lower leg with the other hand which was cold and smooth. As soon as I stopped she looked at me pleadingly and I continued. She was breathing heavily and held my leg harder and harder.

I fill the sink with cold water and go into the kitchen to get some ice that I empty into the water. Look in the mirror.

I stopped wanking five times and every time I stopped she looked at me as if she was about to start crying. Her hand moved faster and faster under the lilac t-shirt. I was sweating and watched the Picasso poster on the wall by the far end of the bed.

I take a deep breath and slowly lower my whole head into the ice cold water and I look at the white bottom of the sink and I can feel an ice cube floating on the surface constantly touching my ear and every time it kind of burns.

She let go of my leg and looked at me and gave me a white cotton handkerchief with some pink letters embroidered on it. She moved her hand faster and faster and groaned submissively between the fast heavy breaths and it sounded like someone was torturing her. She grabbed my leg again. I could feel her nails digging into my skin.

Try to keep my head completely still. Imagine my whole head like a rock in water.

I closed my eyes and listened to the monotonous sounds and her horrible scream. I saw in my head a psychopath slowly beating her back with a sledgehammer and every time she got beaten she let out one of these screaming groans. A few times she let out a quiet sob and I wondered why and tried to see her face in my head but it was impossible no matter how hard I tried. I felt I was about to come. Thought about the Picasso poster. The girl's twisted face and the doll on her lap.

I pull my head quickly out of the water and catch my breath. Look at the ceiling and I black out for a few seconds and I see red dots and breathe heavily. Dry myself with the towel and look at myself in the mirror. Empty the water out and the ice cubes that have half melted.

Leave the bathroom and go over to the bed and sit down.

I can hear the rain and I go into the kitchen and stand by the window and think that someone should really chop those trees down.

Micke calls when I'm having breakfast and wants to know if I want to come along to a party tonight. Some girl in Åkersberga he knows. Her parents are away and the villa is gigantic and loads of people are coming. According to him. I agree to get some coke and he suggests calling Tom but when I've hung up I don't feel like calling him. I finish eating and decide to call Luciano instead. An Italian guy who works in the kitchen at Casa Bianca who I haven't spoken to in months.

'Of course I've got coke, he says when I call and we decide to meet at Casa Bianca around five.

Watch a movie on Filmnet and when it finishes I decide to walk there.

Get fifteen hundred out from the cashpoint at S:t Eriksplan and they've just opened when I get to Casa. The whole restaurant is empty except for a couple by the window. All the staff are sitting by the small tables in the bar and I go up to them.

'Hey, how's it going?' a guy I vaguely know from a party says.

'Hey, yeah cool, you? Is Luciano working?'

'Mmm, sure.' He makes a sweeping gesture towards the kitchen.

I go into the tiny kitchen and say hello to the garde manger who's this extremely ugly redhead girl and walk past the kitchen porter and pat Luciano, who's making some pasta, on the shoulder.

'Hey, it's been a while.' He grins but seems stressed. 'Hey, I'm just making some pasta... do you want some? Puttanesca?'

'Sure that would be nice.'

'Why don't you sit out in the backyard.'

I sit down at the little white plastic table. In the neighbouring backyard the chefs from Rörstrandskrog are having a coffee and they're looking at me and I don't know if I should say hi or not.

After five minutes Luciano comes out and puts a bowl of pasta on the table and dries his hands on the apron and we shake hands.

'How's it going?' he asks and smiles.

'Not bad,' I say.

'Hey come and have a look at this.'

'Sure.'

We walk up to where the bins are kept and he opens the door and picks up a couple of bin bags.

'Check the floor properly. Bend down.'

I squat down and see the fat little maggots wriggling on the metal floor. Luciano laughs and I gag a couple of times.

'We discovered it this afternoon,' he says and we go back to the table and sit down.

'Oh yeah... you might not want your pasta now?'

'No, I don't know. No I don't. I'm also in a bit of a rush,' I lie.

'Damn that's a shame… we have to grab a beer one day.'

'Sure, give me a ring.'

'So you wanted some coke?'

'Yes.' I look over to the other backyard and notice that the chefs have gone back inside.

'Two grams you said.'

'Yes.'

He opens his wallet and out of one of the slots he produces a small envelope that he hands me.

'Eleven hundred?' I ask.

'Yes… that's what I pay.'

'Yes of course, I didn't mean it like that.'

'No worries.'

'Cool,' I say and give him the money.

The redhead garde manger comes out and stands in the doorway.

'You have two tickets,' she screams.

'Yes, for fuck's sake, I'm coming,' he screams back.

We get up and he takes the bowl of pasta and slowly walks back and I follow him.

'A beer one day,' he says when we're inside.

'Sure.'

'Bye.'

What Micke told me earlier in the day was correct. The villa is enormous and we go through it and out into the garden where perhaps fifty people are scattered around. Micke walks over to a girl who's sitting down in a deck chair by the pool with a glass in her hand and I follow. He says hello and introduces us. She's called Elisabeth and has straight blond hair and is fairly pretty. A few girls stand around her and they all have a glass in their hand and smoke long cigarettes and look blasé.

Micke leans forward to this Elisabeth and whispers something in her ear and she giggles. I wonder how old she is? Eighteen? He turns to me and we go back into the house.

We go upstairs and into what is probably some kind of guest room. Micke switches the lights on and says:

'Get the gear out then.'

There's only a handful of people I know at the party but it doesn't really matter. I'm enjoying it. I do a round by myself and check everyone out and say hi to a few. Three four times I go past and stop a few metres away from a girl who's lying face down on a badly inflated air mattress by the pool. She cries uncontrollably and a boy (her boyfriend?) is squatting next to her stroking her hair with one hand. Both are wearing shades and I wonder why she's crying.

Every now and then Micke and I go upstairs for a line.

By two there's only about thirty people left and most have gone inside. When we're not upstairs doing lines we're hanging out with this Elisabeth girl and some of the others in one of the living rooms and watch a cartoon but most people only glance at the screen occasionally whilst a joint is making the rounds. I recognise a girl in the armchair opposite the table. I fucked her at mine after some party I think. Even though we were drunk then and high now we recognise each other but I have absolutely no desire to say hello or talk to her and it seems the feeling is mutual. Next door an old song by Japan is on repeat and one line sticks in my head: "Whatever gets you through the night, just keep on dancing". A guy in the sofa with his arm around Elisabeth keeps going on about wanting to watch Platoon "instead of this shit". She seems pretty annoyed and looks like she wants to tell him to fuck off but she probably doesn't want to ruin her chances of a shag.

When the guy eventually goes up to the video player and takes out the cartoon video and puts on Platoon instead, Micke and I demonstratively go upstairs to finish off the coke. We chop out a fat line each and Micke puts his arm around me and says (he's so high now he's beginning to be annoying):

'Damn it Johan... have you seen Scarface?'

'Yeah.'

'Damn it Johan don't you want to... don't you get that feeling sometimes... do what he does in the end...' He looks out the window with an empty stare and lets out a little laugh between the incoherent sentences. 'Like... this feeling... imagine... damn it... Johan... to not have to care... and just sit there like him... behind this giant desk in this giant villa and let your head sink into this... giant pile of cocaine...'

119

'Johan,' I answer the phone before the second signal.

'Heeey… it's Lisa.'

'Hi… aren't you supposed to be in Paris?'

'Yeah but you know this job, it dragged on and, and there was a casting I just had to go to, so I'm leaving tonight.'

'Oh, I see.'

'The plane leaves at 19.45.'

'Uh-huh.'

'Hey…'

'Yes.'

'Hey… It would make me really happy if you wanted to come with me to the airport… really happy.'

'What about your parents? Don't they want to see you off?'

'Look, I haven't spoken to my dad in two months.' She giggles. 'He's in Brussels or Paris I think and my mum is with me every night at Berns.'

'Uh-huh.'

'Please will you come?'

I can see her huge pleading eyes in front of me.

'Sure.' I really try to sound enthusiastic.

We don't say a word to each other during the forty-five minute bus journey to Arlanda. Nothing. The silence is not embarrassing at all. It somehow feels nice to sit in this big musty brown seat and look at all the computer companies' new buildings passing by the window and have her next to me.

I stand behind her when she checks in and my hands are getting sweaty. When she's handed her luggage in she looks at me and says gate eight.

We're outside the passport control and she starts crying just as I've expected and she does it because she knows she has to.

'Johan,' she sobs.
'Yes.'
'Johan.'
'Yes.'
'Will you come and visit me?'
'I don't know.'
'No of course, how could you?'
'No.'
'No.' She looks at me intensively and pushes her passport through the window and when she's got it back she opens the door next to her and goes through without turning round to look at me and I realise I probably should have said safe travel or good luck or something and then I remember that they have video games in the caff on the second floor. At least they did a year ago.

I head up there and it turns out three of the games are broken and the others seem insanely boring. There's a picture game and a space game called Space Armageddon and a Donkey Kong. I play Donkey Kong once then realise I have no more coins. Since I don't really want to play any more I don't change up any money and leave.

When I'm back on the ground floor I go into the newsagent next to the escalators and buy a Penthouse and when I've paid for it and gone outside I stand next to the bus stop and hold the magazine up with both hands. I slowly rub my fingers over the tanned cover girl. Look at her big and absolutely perfect breasts and when I've caressed the glossy thick smooth cover and her body for a minute or so I hear the bus arriving. A sense of being completely perverted comes over me and I throw the magazine in a bin and get on the bus.

Linda and I are in Café Gateau and it feels like it's the first time in ages I've seen her.

She has a café au lait and I have a juice and we stare at each other a little intensively.

'I don't know but... maybe this sounds awkward but... I feel like I have changed a lot these last months... and I don't mean anything with Anders and that,' she says quite suddenly after we've been quiet a long time. I would usually find this extremely embarrassing but I feel calm and think it's like a scene in a movie where the main character runs into an old childhood friend for the first time in thirty years.

'What do you mean?'

'Well, like... oh, I don't know.' She looks down at the table and I smile a little. 'I mean are you never bored of Hard Rock and... or bored of all that?'

'Yeah of course I am, who wouldn't be?'

'Yeah but I mean, can you see yourself there in a year?'

'No.'

She takes a deep breath.

'No exactly, that's what I mean, one day I think you'll just feel that everything is just passé... you feel really old.'

'Yeah... I don't know, maybe.'

'I think everybody sooner or later becomes so fucking bored of what they're doing and... yes I know it sounds like a cliché.'

'Actually... Yes.' I smile. She smiles.

'Maybe it's obvious...' She stops herself.

We both light a cigarette and she seems to be a little embarrassed about what she's said.

I sit down by myself at Tranan with my pytt i panna and a beer and read an Expressen someone's left behind whilst waiting for Fredrik and Louise and Helene to arrive. Some old James Brown tune is on in the background.

Fredrik arrives and I look at the clock behind the bar that's mirrored and work out it's twenty to nine.

He buys two Ramlösa and sits down.

'Hey, I spoke to an old friend who's just returned from America.'

'Ok.'

'He's been there for a year to study and that and he told me a really cool story. A girl he went out with told it to him.'

'Mmm.'

'So this is a true story... this girl used to go out with a guy and it was this guy's birthday right, and his parents were going away for the weekend... they say bye and that and when his parents have left he calls his girlfriend... this girl who went out with my friend... and she comes over.'

He sips his water and lights a cigarette.

'They sit down on the sofa and start making out and after a while they're completely naked and about to fuck... and they go into... "Le position du chien" you know...'

'Uh?'

'You know... doggy style. They've just started fucking when the phone rings and the girl suggests they try and stay... in the same position whilst he picks up. Sure, cool, the guy says and they start... well... crawling towards the phone and it's his mum on the line. I'm calling from a pay phone by the highway and I think I forgot to turn the stove off before we left, she says. Can you go and check right away, I'm sure I forgot to turn it off. The guy says sure mum I'll check right away. They say have a nice time and all that and hang up. The girl and the guy breathe out and laugh and stay in the same position. The girl says let's try and make it to the stove like this. Sure the guy says.'

He pauses and has a sip of Ramlösa.

'So they stay in position and start crawling towards the kitchen. Crawl, crawl, crawl, puff, pant, gasp. They finally reach the kitchen door and manage to open it with difficulty... and there's the whole family and all the relatives... surprise... his mum made the call from around the corner.'

'Noo...' I say and smile and laugh a little.

'Imagine... what do you do?'

'I'm not sure I believe that.'

'What, really...it's not that unbelievable.'

Louise and Helene arrive and they start drinking beer insanely fast and ask if we want to come along to a party in Döbelnsgatan. Fredrik says he's having a night off and says no.

By eleven I've had three beers and Louise and Helene have had four each and Fredrik says he's splitting and we buy a bottle of wine and leave. When we're outside Fredrik goes to the bus stop at Odenplan and the rest of us head to Helene's who lives above the video shop by the junction of Norrtullsgatan and Surbrunnsgatan.

We sit down on one of her Persian rugs and drink the red wine. Helene lights candles and I feel like I'm in a seventies movie.

My cat allergy comes on just as we've finished drinking the wine.

We get a cab to the party and it turns out it's hosted by some American artist. The only person I recognise is the drummer from Imperiet who walks restlessly back and forth. I get a glass of wine from the kitchen bar and go to the living room and sit down at the longest table I have ever seen. No more than fifteen centimetres high but the top is probably three square metres. The actor Helene was talking about at hers earlier is on a sofa and Helene walks up and is full of admiration and starts hitting on him.

On my way to the loo I pass two guys who are looking at a framed picture of loads of stick figures fucking.

'Damn, not everyone has an original Keith Haring at home,' one of them says.

'Amazing,' the other one says.

It's half one and we've been at this boring party an hour or so and Helene who's not having much luck with the actor (she says she thinks he's gay) suggests we go to some new club in Östermalm.

They get a cab there and I go to McDonald's in Sveavägen and order a fish burger and go home.

I'm waiting for Fredrik and Micke to show up. They called from Hard Rock around five and asked if I wanted to come out when they finished work.

Thinking about getting in the car and going somewhere but change my mind and start looking for that song by Japan I heard at the party a few days ago. "Whatever gets you through the night, just keep on dancing." It sounded like the guy was singing through his teeth when he sang "keep on dancing", emphasis on dancing. Whilst I'm looking (I know I've got it on a 45) I find another single by Roy Orbison. It's called "You got it" and it really is awful. I was given it at some promotion event at Hard Rock. He had just died and the disk jockey kept playing his new record all night.

Manage to break the record in half. Then break it into four. I finally find the single by Japan. "Adolescent Sex" it's called and I turn it on and listen to the lyrics: "The sidewalks trading love as the subway lights grow brighter. We're just another hype and the pressure's getting harder". And then the "Whatever gets you through the night, just keep on dancing".

Fredrik and Micke arrive and we watch some music videos and then decide to head over to Peppar.

I don't know why, but this is the first time Fredrik has ever been at Peppar even though it's been open for months. I can't be bothered finding out why. We have a few beers and Fredrik says the beer glasses look like light bulbs and we laugh and say maybe.

Micke is eyeing up a girl in a black miniskirt at the bar and then turns around to us and says:

'I feel like a proper fucking shag tonight.'

'Mmm, that would be good,' I say and look at Fredrik who puts on some kind of hopeful face.

'Sure. Creml or Göta köttis?'

'Creml... fuck... shall we go there?' Micke asks excitedly as if it were a new amazing place he'd never been to before.

It's drizzling when we get out of the cab in Drottninggatan. We go past the queue and Micke says hi to the bouncer who looks like a rocker. He's wearing a denim jacket, jeans and has a moustache and a gold ring in his pierced ear.

'Hi, there's three of us from Hard Rock. Cool?' He looks through his wallet for his staff-ID.

The bouncer just shakes his head and smiles.

'Guys... It sounds really degrading. First of all you're pretty drunk and you have to be twenty-three to get in and even if you have ID's you're just too drunk.'

'Come on,' Micke says and he actually looks surprised and confused. 'Are you serious?'

The bouncer nods and grins.

'That's outrageous... are you fucking new here?'

The bouncer looks at him wearily and the other bouncer looks ready to interfere. Fredrik and I move away from the entrance and go into a side street. After a minute Micke comes back and he's bright red and kicks the wall.

'What the fuck, who are those idiots on the door?' He screams and looks at the wall he's kicking. 'I've never been so fucking humiliated... last time this happened I was seventeen or something... I don't get it.'

'Come on Micke, you are a bit drunk,' Fredrik says calmly. He doesn't reply.

'It's not the end of the world... they're idiots, ok, so what? Let's forget about them,' he continues.

Micke sighs dismally and looks up at the building and shakes his head.

We're silent for a few minutes and my ears hurt when a police car drives past with its sirens on.

'So, where are we going?' Fredrik finally asks.

'I think I'll just go home and have a solo shag,' Micke says and sounds like he's about to kill himself.

'Me too,' I say.

'Ok.' Fredrik looks disappointed.

We're silent again.

'What about Ritz? Some goth hooker or an acid house cunt?' Micke asks when he's calmed down.

'Mmm,' I say.

'Sure, that's cool, let's go,' Fredrik says.

"Whatever gets you through the night, just keep on dancing..." pops into my head.

I'm in the coffee room smoking and a guy from the bar is sorting out empty bottles next to me and Micke is reading out loud from Aftonbladet about some rape.

Kicki flings the door open and screams:

'What the fuck are you doing Micke? Thirty-five wants to order.'

'Yeah yeah,' he replies excessively slow.

'They've waited more than ten minutes to order.' She's just inside the door and they can't see each other whilst they're talking. 'It's Dag Finn with some girl for fuck's sake.'

'No, stop it... for fuck's sake Kicki, come here.' He sounds very serious. She comes over to the table.

'Is it really him? The singer from Sha-Boom?' He asks in a tone as if he's made a complete fool out of himself.

Kicki realises he's pulling her leg.

'Yes.'

'Can you not go down under the table and suck his cock really hard whilst I finish smoking.'

'God you're so childish.' She leaves.

'I'm so fucking fed up.' Micke slowly gets up and puts the paper down and throws the half-finished cigarette in the bin full of broken glass.

In the evening Fredrik and I are at Micke's and I'm thinking I've always thought freebasing was only for junkies. Either way, here I am in his flat listening attentively to his lecture on freebasing. He's bought a lump of coke that according to him is 95% pure. He puts the lump in a big tablespoon together with some bicarbonate of soda and some water. I get my lighter out and start heating up the spoon from underneath. After a few minutes the coke starts breaking up and Micke removes some small crystals carefully.

I'm wondering what I've agreed to. Feel like a junkie in a social services propaganda film (Johan was a completely normal guy but…).

Oh well, a bit late to change my mind now and Micke puts the glass in front of me. I breathe in deeply… deeply… deeply… one… two… three… four… five… six… seven…

I feel sick and I'm sweating profusely when I get home at nine in the morning. Lie down on the bed with a pumping, thumping, bubbling head and I know I'm not going to be able to sleep until late afternoon or evening. I feel like I'm about to be sick every time I think of last night. I feel like I'm about to be sick when I think about all the speed we had and the wine we drank. I feel like I'm about to be sick when I think about how much freebasing we did.

Remember I already started feeling sick after breathing in the heavy numbing fumes for the fourth time. Remember I sat on the sofa and tried to focus on the TV screen but it was impossible. Remember we were running around naked (dancing?) in Micke's flat.

Remember staring at ourselves in the mirror often and long. Remember Micke asking me if I wanted any Mebumal or Valium or Nembutal or something before I left and I had a couple of Mebumal. Remember watching Micke when he injected the phial of stesolid he bought six months ago.

Feel so rough. Terrible nausea, my body is completely depleted. Blood every time I blow my nose and my head is still completely clear and buzzing. Thinking about loads of unimportant stuff at an incredible speed. Decide to tidy up then do the washing then rearrange the flat.

That's something I used to think about a lot. Stopped doing it more than six months ago. I remember it was at Lisa's some time and we were just sitting there doing nothing between fucking. It was quiet and relaxed and I was probably looking at the Picasso poster. She said: "Have you thought about how so few things mean anything?" I probably kept looking at the Picasso poster and she asked, or more like stated: "Have you ever really cared about me?" I didn't reply. "Have you ever really cared? About anything... really?" I didn't want to look at her and I said: "I don't know." I really didn't know. And she said: "Me neither." It felt good. I really liked that she was honest. It was so simple. We knew where we were with each other and we didn't care. "Me neither."

It was probably only a week or so later when Linda said something similar. We had been fucking and then watched TV and smoked a joint and after the program was finished (I can't remember what program it was, maybe only music videos? Hip hop?) she sat for ages and crumbled hash and tobacco between her finger tips and looked like she didn't know what she was doing. I was lying in bed and looked at myself faintly reflected in the dark TV screen. She said: "You must feel the same way I do... otherwise you wouldn't be sleeping with me." I said nothing. "You must feel that... how shall I put it... LOVE... the whole concept is so stilted, pretentious, it sounds exaggerated but it is... pointless". I still didn't say anything but remembered the situation with Lisa a few weeks earlier. "Otherwise we wouldn't be sleeping with each other", she said and I think I nodded slightly. She looked out the window and lit a cigarette. "I think most people... just... wishful thinking... pretend that they're madly in love, pretend that we...damn it... it's all we do... pretend... pretend everything."

Everything she said, just like Lisa had, made me so incredibly depressed. If we'd been fourteen or something and they had said all those things, well then it had been embarrassing but now she said it with such clarity that, oh I don't know.

When I thought about it afterwards I felt sad for them in a way, that they were simply unhappy people, but they weren't. Then I thought they had only said it because they were bored and fed up and then I stopped caring.

In the dream Linda was cold and her body was hard (I don't know what material, copper?). She always got to the kitchen before me and broke all the plates that I was about to take out. I cried. Micke was dressed in latex and played pinball and laughed and carried see-through binbags full of cocaine.

Get in the car and drive down Sveavägen towards Norrtull. Drive to Albano at hundred and fifty and then I turn around and go back into town. In Östermalm I stop at a kiosk and buy ice cream. Listen to an old Lloyd Cole cassette whilst driving and "Mainstream" starts just as I finish the ice cream. Remember that it was my favourite track on this cassette. "Swimming is easy when you're stuck in the middle of the Mississippi."

When I get home I call Micke to see if he wants to come to the tanning salon.

He comes over at four and we go to the tanning salon next to Tabu, the strip joint. We stop outside the door.

'A friend of a friend knows the guy who runs Tabu, Greger or something, fucking cool guy. Totally doesn't give a shit about all those communist dykes and the like who want to close the place down. He makes so much fucking money.'

'Uh-huh.' I almost say "So what?" but change my mind.

We go into the tanning salon but the blonde girl isn't working.

Madonna's latest is on my headphones when I'm on the bed sweating. I find it hard to relax and occasionally lift my glasses up and squint at the violet light.

It's half five when we get to Hard Rock. I have a Chef's salad and Micke a chiliburger. Carina tells us she got 1,100 kronor in tips the other night and I say the most I've ever had is 800 but then I worked from midday to closing.

A cassette of old '50s songs is playing and Micke tells everybody who passes by to go and change the tape but everybody replies do it yourself. In the kitchen two chefs are talking about which guitarist is the best, Eddie Van Halen or Yngwie Malmsteen.

'What the fuck, it's all about having both the technical skills and the right feeling. Eddie is perfectly balanced,' says one of them who I think is called Christer.

'Yngwie is in a different class, people don't understand the feeling he has,' the other one says.

I think about when Yngwie Malmsteen was on holiday in Sweden. He was at Hard Rock almost every day with John Norum and those guys. He was so incredibly drunk and high and such a swine.

Remember he was on Micke's table once and he complained about everything and was so rude and said that Micke was a useless waiter and loads of stuff. Every five minutes he'd "spill" something and ordered Micke to wipe it up.

In the end Yngwie gave him a twenty kronor tip and Micke said: "I don't want your disgusting money" and put the two coins down his empty beer glass. Yngwie lost his temper and turned into a lunatic and was going to kill him. The bouncers came to try and calm him down. They couldn't throw him out (or had orders not to). Apparently Hard Rock was the only place he wasn't barred from. He really was a pig. Used to break chairs and pour the contents of the salt shaker onto the tables and half his beer on top so it all turned into mush. Then he'd call the waitress who had to try and clean it up. For months after he had returned to America all the staff talked about stuff he'd done and how drunk he'd been and how high every time he'd been here.

I remember being hugely relieved I never had his table.

Check the schedule. Carina and Anders are on until ten. Helene and Micke until midnight. Me and Fia until closing.

Fredrik calls around two and asks if I want to come along to the preview of a film called Dead Calm. Martin is handing out free tickets to the staff. Fredrik tells me to get down there for five.

I manage to blag some staff food even though I'm not working. Sit down to eat and drink coffee whilst I'm waiting for the others to finish. Micke's going around with a list putting everyone's name down who wants some ecstasy for the staff party in a few weeks. Apparently he's been offered to buy some but he has to buy at least ten, so he's asking everyone who might be interested.

There's about ten of us from Hard Rock meeting outside the cinema at quarter to seven.

The film is not particularly good, even though I jump in my seat a couple of times. Afterwards when we're out in the street Micke says he thought it was shit.

'I thought it was great,' Fredrik says (to be contrary?) and smiles at him.

'What the fuck, for one, you could tell the dead bodies were dolls. That's really annoying.'

'Just use your imagination, you know,' Fredrik smiles teasingly.

'Ok, there was one really cool thing. When that bloke got the flare in his gob and light came out of all the holes in his head. Fucking cool.' He smiles to himself and nods slightly. Fucking cool.

We go to Downtown but halfway there we change our minds.

'Saatan perkelä. Large beer is twenty-two kronor. Vodka. I want a Koskenkorva,' Micke says in a Finnish accent and beats his chest. 'Only people like that go there, apart from when it's people working in a bank or whoever they are.'

'I think it's mainly country bumpkins,' Fredrik says.

'Ok, but surely drunk Finns are country bumpkins aren't they?'

I nod.

Fredrik laughs.

We head over to Norrmalmstorg to get the bus and on our way there Micke tells us two of his worst jokes.

'Three guys went camping. They lay down next to each other to go to sleep. In the morning when they woke up… no, wait, have you heard this one? Fucking great! Those pathologists, you know, that murder when the victim was butchered and all that. Right, so these two pathologists have just finished dinner at Caféet and there's only one thing missing and one of them says to the other: "Do you want to go HALVES on a hooker?" So fucking funny!' We laugh. 'But, anyway, the campers… they woke up in the morning and the guy on the far left said: "Check this guys, I had an amazing dream, some really hot chick was jerking me off." The one on the right says: "No shit, I had the

same dream, that a really gorgeous girl was jerking me off."
The guy in the middle says: "I dreamt I was cross-country
skiing."

'It's definitely summer. Micke is wearing a new pair of aviator sunglasses and smiles at me. His hair is carelessly combed and it's shiny with gel and he constantly runs his hand through it. We're on two rocks next to each other and we've just shared a joint and it's half ten and it's still light. I'm drinking Stella and Micke's drinking Kangaroo and we're a bit outside the ring around the fire. Helene is on a tree stump with her arms around some guy who's got one hand inside her jumper. There's probably around fifteen twenty of us and the temperature is mild and there's almost no wind. A slow song by The Bangles is playing on the cassette player and it's relaxed even though most of us are a bit drunk and coming up on pills. Two barefoot girls are by the water giggling. One of them has a bob and an oversized cotton shirt with some green and red inca pattern on that comes halfway down her tight black bike shorts. Micke takes his shades off and hangs them from the white vest he's wearing underneath an unbuttoned black leather jacket. He pulls a packet of Prince and a lighter out of one of his pockets.

'You fancy her?' His eyes are pointing in the direction of the girl.

He could be talking about her friend but I don't think so.

'Don't know.'

'Don't know?'

'Don't know… well, yeah.'

'I think she's called Lotta. Amazing in bed… Like an animal.'

'Have you fucked her?'

'Mmm, long time ago.' He exhales slowly and stares blankly in front of him. 'I think they're coming up on the Blue Dragon Steve gave them.'

I'm wondering who Steve is but imagine it's one of the guys I don't know by the fire. Can't be bothered asking.

'So you're going for it again or what?' I ask and try to smile.

'Mmm, I don't know… knowing her it wouldn't be a problem.'

A guy in a turquoise shirt and shades on his forehead comes up to us and squats in front of Micke. I'm wondering if this is Steve? He grins and has an empty stare. He smiles feebly and seems high and looks at Micke and asks if we want some weed.

Micke glances at me and then looks at this guy who's nodding along with the music and smiles and squints at him.

'You know what, I think we're fine, but thanks for asking.'

'Sure, sure, cool, no worries, cool.' He says it slowly and grins between each word and sounds really dopey. He gets up and goes back and sits down again. A girl reaches towards the cassette player and turns it up. Some song by

INXS. Her and two other girls who are all good-looking start dancing half-heartedly.

The girl in the bike shorts (Lotta?) and her friend start dancing towards them. The whole thing feels a bit silly and embarrassing when you're not that high yourself. Micke and I are kind of a couple of outsiders here, especially as we're a few metres away from everyone else. Helene and that guy start rolling around in the sand and giggle and Micke starts rolling a fat one.

'Damn, we have to catch up, we should really be on the Blue Dragon but… if not, we might as well leave.'

'Then let's, I say.'

'Which one? Catch up or leave?'

'Yeah… catch up.' I look over at Lotta who's drinking big gulps of wine straight from the bottle of white (Green Pearl?) and she looks at me and smiles when she's put the bottle down. Micke lights the joint and has a few drags than passes it to me. We're the only ones still sitting down apart from the ones passed out in the sand or semi fucking.

Steve and two girls have gone to the parking lot and sat down in his Porsche and next to it is a BMW and some people are talking.

We finish smoking and go over to where the people are dancing. It's a slow song and Micke hugs Lotta's friend who's actually really pretty close up. They cuddle each other and wobble and giggle. I feel a bit left out and a bit confused and a bit high and I look at Lotta who's sat down. Her hair is tousled and she's holding the bottle of wine in both hands. She gives me a look and nods slightly and it can't mean anything but come and sit here. I hope.

145

'Do you want some?' She hands me the bottle and looks at me.

'Thanks.'

'Now hold me... I'm cold.' She stares at the water and smiles absentmindedly.

I put one arm around her and she pulls me towards her and the bottle falls over and I can hear the wine pouring out whilst we're kissing and it feels pretty good. She's shivering slightly but I don't think she's cold at all, only lonely and horny and high.

When I've finished breakfast and read the paper I stand by the kitchen window and smoke. The trees are simply trees. No arms, no bodies.

Get the Lloyd Cole cassette from the car. Fast forward to "Mainstream": "When am I ever going to kick the curse? I took my medication and I feel worse. Swimming is easy when you're stuck in the Mississippi." And the second chorus: "Swimming is easy when you're headed for the deep."

Realise I've had the same message on my answering machine for more than a month. Listen to it: "Hi it's Johan but I'm out. Say something after the beep."

Decide to record a new one.

Press record and say: "Hi you've reached Johan. I'm currently out but at some point I'll return. If you have something to say to me do so after the beep."

Listen to it: "Hi you've reached Johan. I'm currently out but at some point I will return. If you have something to say to me do so after the beep." Listen to it again "…I'm currently out but at some point I will return…"

At Hard Rock Carina and Helene are at the counter giggling and talking about some guy they've both fucked.

I say hi and sit down next to them. They ask if I know someone called Joakim and I say no and they say good and start giggling again. I read the first page of Expressen which is partly about the murder of Palme, partly about the murder of a woman. Helene gets a mirror out and checks her mascara. Carina lights a cigarette and says another night in this fucking place. Helene puts her mirror back and has a sip of coffee and lights a cigarette.

I felt nothing. Absolutely nothing. I lit a match and let it burn until I nearly burned myself. Looked at the burnt out match, distorted. My fingers white, pale, pale yellow, almost as thin as cigarettes. Lit the cigarette and took a deep breath. That noise and pale light around me seemed almost like total silence. I smoked slowly, long deep drags and watched with an empty stare as the glow slowly ate the tobacco. The feeling that everything around me moved so quickly that everything was still, or the other way around? A feeling of being restless and yet still. A kind of flicker. Some videos had the same feeling. Some pictures I remembered stayed with me, very close in a way.

I felt nothing, absolutely nothing.

and I

Also by Nordisk Books

Havoc
Tom Kristensen

*You can't betray your best friend
and learn to sing at the same time*
Kim Hiorthøy

Love/War
Ebba Witt-Brattström

Zero
Gine Cornelia Pedersen

Termin
Henrik Nor-Hansen

Transfer Window
Maria Gerhardt

Inlands
Elin Willows

Restless
Kenneth Moe

We'll Call You
Jacob Sundberg

Fixed Ideas
Eline Lund Fjæren

Speed of Life
Michael Strunge